D1534979

FLAT LINE

J.M. MADDEN

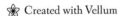

For my Family, as always. You know I love you.

This is one of the funnest sets I've ever worked on. The other authors have been fantastic and Becky McGraw has been especially remarkable.

While these books can all be read as standalones, we hope that you will read them all. Every author in this set I have read before, and I will again because I love their styles.

If you think you've missed one of the twelve, you can follow this Link to my website for a complete list.

www.jmmadden.com/sleeper-seals/

And of course if you have any questions you can email me any time at authorjmmadden@gmail.com

RETIRED NAVY COMMANDER Greg Lambert leaned
forward to rake in the pile of chips his full house had netted
him. Tonight he would leave the weekly gathering not only
with his pockets full, but his pride intact.

The scowls he earned from his poker buddies at his
unusual good luck were an added bonus.

They'd become too accustomed to him coming up on
the losing side of five card stud. It was about time he taught
them to never underestimate him.

Vice President Warren Angelo downed the rest of his
bourbon and stubbed out his Cuban cigar. "Looks like Lady
Luck is on your side tonight, Commander."

After he stacked his chips neatly in a row at the rail in
front of him, Greg glanced around at his friends. It occurred
to him right then, this weekly meeting wasn't so different
from the joint sessions they used to have at the Pentagon
during his last five years of service.

The location was the Secretary of State's basement now,
but the gathering still included top ranking military brass,

politicians, and the director of the CIA, who had been staring at him strangely all night long.

"It's about time the bitch smiled my way, don't you think? She usually just cleans out my pockets and gives you my money," Greg replied with a sharp laugh as his eyes roved over the spacious man-cave with envy, before they snagged on the wall clock.

It was well past midnight, their normal break-up time. He needed to get home, but what did he have to go home to? Four walls, and Karen's mean as hell Chihuahua who hated him. Greg stood, scooted back his chair, and stretched his shoulders. The rest of his poker buddies left quickly, except for Vice President Angelo, Benedict Hughes of the CIA, and their host, Percy Long, Secretary of State.

Greg took the last swig of his bourbon, then set the glass on the table. When he took a step to leave, they moved to block his way to the door. "Something on your minds, gentleman?" he asked, their cold, sober stares making the hair on the back of his neck stand up.

It wasn't a comfortable feeling, but one he was familiar with from his days as a Navy SEAL. That feeling usually didn't portend anything good was about to go down. But neither did the looks on these men's faces.

Warren cleared his throat and leaned against the mahogany bar with its leather trimmings. "There's been a significant amount of chatter lately." He glanced at Ben. "We're concerned."

Greg backed up a few steps, putting some distance between himself and the men. "Why are you telling me this? I've been out of the loop for a while now." Greg was retired, and bored stiff, but not stiff enough to tackle all that was wrong in the United States at the moment or fight the politics involved in fixing things.

Ben let out a harsh breath then gulped down his glass of water. He set the empty glass down on the bar with a sigh and met Greg's eyes. "We need your help, and we're not going to beat around the bush," he said, making the hair on Greg's neck stand taller.

Greg put his hands in his pockets, rattling the change in his right pocket and his car keys in the left while he waited for the hammer. Nothing in Washington, D.C., was plain and simple anymore. Not that it ever had been.

"Spit it out, Ben," he said, eyeballing the younger man. "I'm all ears."

"Things have changed in the US. Terrorists are everywhere now," he started, and Greg bit back a laugh at the understatement of the century.

He'd gotten out before the recent INCONUS attacks started, but he was in service on 9/11 for the ultimate attack. The day that replaced Pearl Harbor for him as the day that would go down in infamy.

"That's not news, Ben," Greg said, his frustration mounting in his tone. "What does that have to do with me, other than being a concerned citizen?"

"More cells are being identified every day," Ben replied, his five o'clock shadow standing in stark contrast to his now paler face. "The chatter about imminent threats, big jihad events that are in the works, is getting louder every day."

"You do understand that I'm no longer active duty, right?" Greg shrugged. "I don't see how I can be of much help there."

"We want you to head a new division at the CIA," Warren interjected. "Ghost Ops, our own sleeper cell of SEALs to help us combat the terrorist sleeper cells in the US...and whatever the hell else might pop up later."

Greg laughed. "And where do you think I'll find these SEALs to sign up? Most are deployed over--"

"We want *retired* SEALs like yourself. We've spent millions training these men, and letting them sit idle stateside while we fight this losing battle alone is just a waste." Ben huffed a breath. "I know they'd respect you when you ask them to join the contract team you'd be heading up. You'd have a much better chance of convincing them to help."

"Most of those guys are like me, worn out to the bone or injured when they finally give up the teams. Otherwise, they'd still be active. SEALs don't just quit." *Unless their wives were taken by cancer and their kids were off at college, leaving them alone in a rambling house when they were supposed to be traveling together and enjoying life.*

"What kind of threats are you talking about?" Greg asked, wondering why he was even entertaining such a stupid idea.

"There are many. More every day. Too many for us to fight alone," Ben started, but Warren held up his palm.

"The president is taking a lot of heat. He has three and a half years left in his term, and taking out these threats was a campaign promise. He wants the cells identified and the terror threats eradicated quickly."

These two, and the president, sat behind desks all day. They'd never been on a field op before, so they had no idea the planning and training that took place before a team ever made it to the field. Training a team of broken-down SEALs to work together would take double that time because each knew better than the rest how things should be done, so there was no "quick" about it.

"That's a tall order. I can't possibly get a team of twelve men on the same page in under a year. Even if I can find them." Why in the hell was he getting excited, then? "Most are probably out enjoying life on a beach somewhere." Exactly where he would be with Karen if she hadn't fucking died on him as soon as he retired four years ago.

"We don't want a *team*, Greg," Percy Long corrected, unfolding his arms as he stepped toward him. "This has to be done stealthily because we don't want to panic the public. If word got out about the severity of the threats, people wouldn't leave their homes. The press would pump it up until they created a frenzy. You know how that works."

"So let me get this straight. You want individual SEALs, sleeper guys who agree to be called up for special ops to perform solo missions?" Greg asked, his eyebrows lifting. "That's not usually how they work."

"Unusual times call for unusual methods, Greg. They have the skills to get it done quickly and quietly," Warren replied, and Greg couldn't argue. That's exactly the way SEALs were trained to operate--they did whatever it took to get the job done.

Ben approached him, placed his hand on his shoulder as if this was a tag-team effort, and Greg had no doubt that it was just that. "Every terrorist or wannabe terror organization has roots here now. Al Qaeda, the Muslim Brotherhood, Isis, or the Taliban, white supremacists and other armed hate groups--you name it. They're not here looking for asylum. They're actively recruiting followers and planning events to create a caliphate on our home turf. We can't let that happen, Greg, or the United States will never be the same."

"You'll be a CIA contractor, and can name your price," Warren inserted, and Greg's eyes swung to him. "You'll be on your own in the decision making. We need to have plausible deniability if anything goes wrong."

"Of course," Greg replied, shaking his head. If anything went south, they needed a fall guy, and that would be him in this scenario. Not much different from the dark ops his teams performed under his command when he was active duty.

God, why did this stupid idea suddenly sound so intriguing? Why did he think he might be able to make it work? And why in the hell did he suddenly think it was just what he needed to break out of the funk he'd been living in for four years?

"I can get you a list of potential hires, newly retired SEALs, and the president says *anything* else you need," Warren continued quickly. "All we need is your commitment."

The room went silent, and Greg looked deeply into each man's eyes as he pondered a decision. What the hell did he have to lose? If he didn't agree, he'd just die a slow, agonizing death in his recliner at home. At only forty-seven and still fit, that could be a lot of years spent in that chair.

"Get me the intel, the list, and the contract," he said, and a surge of adrenaline made his knees weak.

He was back in the game.

CHAPTER 1

PARKER QUINN DIDN'T RECOGNIZE the number, but he did recognize the area code and a bolt of something exciting jerked through him. Who in that exclusive Virginia area code would be calling him? It had been a long time since he'd seen a number like that.

Curiosity won out and he swiped his thumb across the screen and brought it to his ear. "Hello?"

"Quinn! How the hell are you, buddy?"

Parker scowled and looked at the phone, wondering if he'd fallen into some type of time warp. It had been a couple of years since he'd spoken with his former boss, Navy SEAL Commander Greg Lambert, but he remembered his voice like it had been yesterday. "Hello, sir."

Parker had no idea why the man was calling him now. After he'd been injured, Lambert had been in to see him once, then never again.

Probably couldn't stand to be reminded what could happen when he looked at me.

That wasn't a very charitable thought, but it was how he'd felt at the time. Hurt and left behind. He'd given a huge amount of his life and sanity for his country, and his team, but as soon as he was damaged and no longer usable they were done with him. Yeah, they paid him his hazard bonus but, whatever.

He waited for Lambert to speak, because he wasn't sure how he felt about even talking to the man.

After a couple of long seconds, Lambert cleared his throat. "Well, I wanted to check up on you, see how you'd recovered."

Scowling, Parker looked out over the parking lot. He heard papers rustle in the background and had a feeling Lambert was looking at his medical record—if he wasn't actually watching him. The man had friends in high places with expensive toys. And Lambert never asked rhetorical questions. "I'm fine, thank you. As you can see."

His former boss chuckled. "You always did like to call me on my shit, Quinn. I appreciated that about you. Tell me what I can't read in the medical file. There's not much here."

Parker shook his head and looked around, suddenly overwhelmed with anger. They'd wiped their hands of him, now they wanted him to bleed for them again. "What's not in the file? It's not in the file that I can't take too deep of a breath because one of my ribs pops, and doctors can't tell me why. It's not in the file that it takes me twenty minutes to clear my eye socket of goop every morning. It's not in the file that my dick bends to the right when I get hard because of all the scar tissue on my lower belly. Is that what you're looking for Lambert? Some other reason to feel like you have it good in life? Why the fuck are you calling me?"

Silence stretched on the other end of the line and Parker realized he might have gone overboard. That banked anger that he'd learned to control had flared to life. He was almost yelling, and that wouldn't get either one of them anywhere.

"I'm sorry, Parker," Lambert said eventually. "No, I'm not calling you to make myself feel better. Since my wife died those moments are few and far between, so I'll have to think about our conversation later and see if it perks me up and makes me feel all sparkly inside."

Parker snorted in spite of himself. Lambert was as much of an asshole as he'd always been.

"How's your mobility?"

Again, Parker scowled. His mobility was a touchy subject. "Fine," he lied. "Why?"

Lambert sighed on the other end of the line. "I know you've gotten a job in Denver with Duncan Wilde, but I don't know what you're doing."

"Why don't you call him and snoop, like you used to? Use your influence to strong arm him into telling you?"

"I thought about it but I'm giving you the option of telling me. You were a good SEAL Quinn, and I'm sorry you got rolled out the way you did. I didn't follow up with you the way I should have, but if you're like me, you're chafing in the civilian world, looking for something more. I've got something for you but you have to be physically able to do it."

He wasn't even sure he wanted whatever it was. Probably some do or die mission that had to be acted upon immediately. That was usually the way Greg Lambert worked. And if Parker didn't do the job, Lambert would call some other dumb schmuck who would.

He had a good life here in Denver. After he'd been released from the SEALs, medically retired from the Navy, he'd moped for a long time, and wallowed in his recovery. Physically, he'd been mobile, but just barely. The insurgents had done a real number on him. When word had gotten around to him that there was a former Marine in Denver that only hired other disabled veterans, he'd been intrigued, but not much more than that. It wasn't until months later that he actually looked the place up online. There was one tab on the website to 'apply to join our team!' Parker hadn't even had a resume at the time. How do you encapsulate thirteen years in the Navy and all his SEAL experience into a few paragraphs? You didn't, you couldn't; most of his missions had been classified and he couldn't discuss them with anyone, ever. Instead he'd left his former commander's name and number, as well as a copy of his medical record. Apparently that had worked because a woman from Lost and Found called him two weeks later to arrange an interview, if he was still interested in the job.

Was he? He'd looked around his neglected apartment and knew he needed something to get him out of the slump he was in, so he'd agreed.

It was the best thing he'd ever done. The Lost and Found Investigative Service was comprised of veterans just like him-- men that had seen the bad side of war and returned from it changed. There were also a few women vets working there, just as blunt and capable as the men. Duncan Wilde had proven to be a savvy boss, pushing him to the limits of what he could do but not taxing him too much. Generally, he did surveillance or he drove clients that were under their protection. Denver wasn't a metropolis like New York or LA, but they had their fair share of affluent people needing coverage. He'd gotten his private investigator's license and realized that the more he got into the job, the more he had to learn. It was giving him something to work toward.

Parker didn't mind the challenge. It gave him something

to focus on. Yes, it could have been more stimulating, but he understood that he needed to start on the bottom, too, and work his way up to the meatier jobs.

"The pay is substantial."

When Lambert spewed out the number, Parker couldn't keep the surprise from his face. "That's a heck of a teaser. What's the job?"

"Surveillance, for the most part, and possibly more. You'll be sitting on a prosecuting attorney for the next week. She's the primary in a criminal case against an actor from a small terror cell in Columbus, Ohio. He had visions of being a lone wolf but botched the job. Now he's in lockup awaiting trial. Actually, we think Mozi Al Fareq is the fourth or fifth son of the man that runs the terrorist cell responsible for the truck attack on the Columbus Christmas Parade several months ago. Do you remember that?"

"Of course," Parker said softly. "It killed a lot of people, mostly kids."

"Yes," Lambert said, his voice muted. "Fuckers. There's a special place in hell for people who kill little kids like that."

They were both silent for a long moment, each lost in their own thoughts.

"The cell has direct links through social media to known Islamic State operatives, but they've stayed quiet about this particular attack that al Fareq botched. Some of our experts think al Fareq was chafing under his father's thumb and decided to make a name for himself with a big splashy suicide, but it didn't work out that way. He didn't die when he drove that truck down the sidewalk at the art fair, then crashed into the Center of Science and Industry building. A security guard tased him when Mozi tried to shoot people outside the museum as he escaped."

Parker snorted. "Great for his ego, I'm sure, being brought down by a security guard like that."

"Well, I don't care about his ego, just the fact that his plans were botched. There were injuries, but it could have been much worse. But al Fareq is realizing how screwed he is and last week he wrote his father a letter pleading for help. We're monitoring all of this, of course, as well as all of his contacts outside."

"It sounds like you have everything under control."

"Not exactly. The father, along with the rest of his cell, has dropped off the grid. We can't find him. Any of them. One of the witnesses in the case has turned up dead, beheaded. Mozi's father, Ali al Fareq, is apparently trying to silence anyone that saw his son get out of the truck. Or just plain unbalance the prosecution's case against his son. Your job will be to protect the prosecutor and if the situation presents itself, take out the cell. You have carte blanche to eliminate everyone connected to this little party."

Parker choked out a laugh. "You're not asking for much."

"I know this is a lot to ask of you, but things are heating up in the states. All of these little cells are honing their skills, *possibly* in preparation of a nationwide, simultaneous attack. We can't have it. We've been authorized by the highest level of government to make these cells go away, any way we can, but if we're caught, they'll disavow all knowledge of what we were doing."

"What?" He stalked across the room. "You've got to be kidding. Why the fuck would I sign up for this? It's a suicide mission."

Lambert sighed on the other end. "I know it feels like that, Quinn, but you have one of the best records of any SEAL I've seen in the past twenty years. You survived more dead end situations than I've seen any other man survive, and single-handedly brought down more terrorist cells than any two squads put together. You have a nose for this stuff and I wouldn't push you to get out there if I didn't think you could handle it."

"What kind of back-up will I have?"

"Nothing official. If you get into a pickle I might be able to have someone help you out. No guarantees."

"Fuck," Parker breathed. "This really is a suicide mission. The money is nice but not if I'm not going to be here to spend it. This is a no-go for me, Lambert. You're going to have to find another lamb to lead to slaughter."

"I need you to reconsider, Quinn. Your country needs you to do this."

Anger swirled through his gut. "Fuck the patriotic bull-shit, Greg. I gave *everything* to this country for thirteen years of my life. I'm not going to give it my death as well. Some other, younger kid looking for glory can do that."

"I need you on this, Quinn," Lambert snapped. "I have other men but they're scattered across the country, doing jobs just like this one. I have an immediate need for coverage, and you are the only man for the job."

Parker shook his head. "I don't understand why you think that. I know for a fact there are other SEALs out there that would love to do this. I'm not the only man for the job."

Greg sighed heavily on the other end of the line. "The prosecuting attorney on the case is Andromeda Pierce."

Shock rolled through Parker and he went still, all of the anger suddenly rolling out of him.

Andromeda.

The years rolled back and he could see her in his mind's eye, long silky dark hair swinging over her shoulder, golden leopard's eyes glinting with intelligence. The last time he'd seen her she had dumped him, then walked away as if she hadn't a care in the world and hadn't just ripped his heart out.

"That's dirty, Lambert."

"I know, Quinn. I'm sorry. If I could have anyone else do this, I would, but you're it for now. It's surprisingly hard finding retired SEALs of your caliber."

Parker shook his head at the ridiculous compliment. "Send me the information and I'll catch a flight out tonight."

"It's on your front doorstep. I'll be in touch, Quinn."

Parker flew Lambert the bird and the older man chuckled as he hung up.

CHAPTER 2

THE SILENCE in the office eventually made her look up. Oh, damn. Had everyone gone home?

Vaguely she remembered Janie calling out a 'later', but she'd been so absorbed in this file that Andromeda couldn't even remember if she'd looked up or waved.

It wasn't like she hadn't read the file before. She had. Many times, in fact, but it drew her back time and again. Each time she cracked it open she had to look at the list of children's names on the upper right-hand corner, clipped there exactly for that reason. She knew she needed to regard them as victims, but for some reason with this case she hadn't been able to find that professional distance. Every child was as familiar to her as if he or she were part of Andromeda's own family. Liam Johnson had loved Legos and building things. As had Noah Green. Lucas had been Noah's friend, there at the Christmas Parade just to go with his buddy to the Children's Expression Workshop. Lily and Aria, twins with curly hair and big brown eyes, had just moved into the area. Their mother had thought the Columbus Parade would be a great way to learn about the city. Auburn haired Charlotte was a little older, almost ten, and she'd been excited to be one of the returning helpers for the Children's Workshop. Ethan was the son of the woman that ran the workshop and he was a bright, smiling, well-grounded child. Muhammed wouldn't have been there at all if his father hadn't had to work that day. His sitter had thought it would be a nice excursion for the two of them.

Nine children gone in the blink of an eye. Some of their siblings and parents had been injured as well, but this particular group of children had been sitting at a table together, working on a Christmas art project. If the semi had veered to the left or right just a few feet, it would have missed their table, but the driver had targeted them specifically. Not those children individually, just a group of children in general.

Now, they had a chance to prosecute the vile human being that had planned the attack, assuming Mozi al Fareq valued his life over his family's honor.

Mozi had tried to commit a similar attack at the Columbus Art Fair just two months ago. He'd gotten his Commercial Driver's License and been hired on at a small transport company based in Springfield, Ohio, about sixty miles away. Mozi's employer had had no qualms about hiring the man. There'd been nothing on his resume to send up a flag and all of his references had checked out. The employees he'd worked with said that he was a quiet guy, but happy to have a job to help out his family. They never expected him to disappear with a truck and try to commit mass murder.

The terroristic MO of the Art Fair attack was very similar to the Christmas Parade attack; so similar, in fact that the prosecutor's office believed the two incidents were connected and they were doing their damnedest to prosecute the hell out of the case. If Mozi wanted to go to court for the Art Fair attack, they would do it, but Andromeda was still holding out hope that he would accept the plea agreement they'd sent his lawyer, and give them what they needed to prosecute *both* cases.

If Mozi gave them the details about the parade attack as well as who had perpetrated it, details about the terror ring he was involved in, he would get a more lenient sentence in his own case. As it stood, Andromeda's case was damn near air tight. She had a handful of witnesses, as well as footage of Mozi driving the truck on a traffic cam downtown before the fair.

If he was smart he would take the plea agreement and start singing like a bird. It was up to him though.

Andromeda pinched the bridge of her nose, feeling the tiredness in her bones. They were getting close to going to court and she'd been putting in more hours than any of the other prosecutors. Not because she had to, but because she wanted justice for the children that had been targeted. They'd been at a damn art fair, for God's sake. A place where they should not have had to worry about their safety. Same with the kids that had died at the Christmas parade.

No one had died at the art fair, but she was prosecuting Mozi for 32 counts of attempted murder, terroristic threats, inducing panic, criminal assault, criminal trespass, and a slew of other violations. She was throwing everything she could think of at him. If convicted he would be serving several life sentences.

These terrorist incidents were happening more and more often, and the perpetrators didn't seem to care who they hurt.

This was a common refrain in her brain and she needed to get out of it. Closing the physical file she crossed to the file cabinet and locked it inside. Then she returned to her laptop and shut it down as well, slid it into the gray suede sleeve, closed the magnetic flap and put it into her leather messenger bag at her side. She straightened her desk, dropping pens and clips where they needed to be. There were a few pieces of outgoing mail she needed to drop onto her assistant's desk on the way out.

Slipping her arms into her hip length brown leather coat, she looked out the window at the gray sky. It wasn't raining at the moment, but it had been on and off all day. Such crappy weather. Matched her mood perfectly.

Andromeda shouldered her bag and grabbed up the mail and her keyring. Turning, she locked her office door behind her as she left and set the mail on Janie's desk. She scanned the office as she walked toward the elevator, but it seemed completely quiet. And lonely. People always left early on Fridays and they were getting into the part of the year when there would be more get-togethers. Halloween was just around the corner, then Thanksgiving. Holidays she would undoubtedly work through.

It had been almost ten months since the parade attack and no one had been arrested. That was so wrong. Someone other than the still unidentified driver who'd died in the fiery crash had to know something. Families, neighbors, it didn't matter who came forward with the information they needed. Someone who'd *seen* something needed to *say* something and the person responsible for that crime was going *down*. If Mozi al Fareq would talk and confirm all their suppositions, they could wrap both cases up together.

Because they were losing witnesses.

The first witness they'd lost had been an older gentleman that had been sweeping the streets blocked off for the art fair. He'd seen everything as it happened. But somehow, just one month before they took Mozi to trial, the street sweeper's life had been lost when a car plowed into him on the street.

Andromeda knew things like that happened, but really, what were the chances?

The next witness she'd lost had been the mother of one of the children injured in the art fair attack, Tandy. Toni Mathers had loved her daughter and had been very vocal about seeing justice be served; hence, the reason she'd come forward to say that she'd seen Mozi get out of the truck with a gun in his hand. So, when she'd committed suicide in her garage something had seemed off. So far, the Medical Examiner had only come out with a 'suspicious' cause of death.

Andromeda had spoken with and liked Toni Mathers. The woman had seemed grounded and determined, the type unwilling to throw her life away, but who was to say?

The deaths were too convenient, though. In all her years of prosecuting scum, she'd never had anyone this ... connected. He had people in all the right places looking out for him, and it was frustrating her to pieces. She had two other viable witnesses for court. One was a cop and the other a man that just happened to be in the right place at the right time.

The elevator chimed softly when it reached her floor and she stepped inside. If she could have brought the semi driver back from the dead she would have, just to question him about his connections and who had helped him plan the heinous Christmas crime. That was outside of her abilities though. She could only do the best she could with what she had.

Mozi knew about that attack, though. She'd questioned him three times and each time she asked him about it he got this smug smile on his face, like it was funny watching her spin her wheels. It was up to Andromeda to find his pressure point. Mozi al Fareq considered it his destiny to go to jail for what he'd done. He would protect the ones around him with every fiber of his being.

What Mozi didn't know was that Andromeda had plans to bury him in the farthest, dirtiest prison corner she could find away from Columbus after she got him convicted.

But she only had five days to do it.

The elevator dinged and she walked out into the underground parking garage. Even the garage was almost empty. She glanced around just to be safe, and waved at the parking attendant in the far corner booth, then she headed for her SUV.

The hairs on the back of her neck suddenly stood at attention, making her feel like she was being watched. Glancing around, she didn't see anyone, but there were plenty of places someone could hide. Hurrying a little, she reached her vehicle and disengaged the locks. She tossed her bag across the far seat as she climbed in and pressed the start button. Then she glanced around. Nothing that she could see but something had stirred her instincts.

Andromeda was a strong believer in listening to the signals your body and your mind gave you. Women were raped or abused all too often because they didn't listen to that warning voice of self-protection deep inside. Mothers who got up in the middle of the night to check on their children earned her respect. Fathers who checked on their kids' Facebook pages because something felt off needed to be commended. She wished everyone would listen to their instincts as well.

Waving at the parking attendant, she turned left on South High Street, then left on Main. Her condo was only a few blocks away, but it was worth it to her to drive. Today, especially. A cold rain pelted down onto the windshield and the wipers were struggling to keep up with it. Leaning forward on her seat, she peered into the foggy glass, looking for her turn. There it was. The bright white sign of Waterford Condominiums loomed into view. Luckily, her building also had an underground garage, vital when you built downtown and space had to be used effectively.

The parking garage was wet but only from other cars that had entered. She paused long enough for the camera to read her vehicle tag before the white metal gate lifted. She accelerated into the garage and circled around to her parking spot. Then, turning the vehicle, she backed into the space, a trick an old friend had ingrained into her.

Gathering her bag and the coffee cup from the center console she stepped out of the car. The parking garage was somewhat protected but a chill wind still managed to blow up her skirt as she headed for the elevator, making her shudder. Maybe it was time to dig out some wool pants from the back of her closet.

She swiped her residency card to call the elevator. Almost immediately the doors slid open.

An electronic screen in the right-hand corner of the elevator showed her Hampton Squires, the guard currently manning the security station somewhere in the depths of the tower. Andromeda had read an article recently about your name influencing what you did in life. She wondered if Hampton had read it.

"Hello, Ms. Pierce. Another late one, huh?"

Andromeda grinned. "Yes, Hampton. I have a big case going to trial next week."

"Well, you go in and get settled and if you need anything you give me a ring."

"Will do. Thank you, Hampton."

Andromeda watched the numbers tick by until it stopped on twenty-seven. Not the top of the high rise— she couldn't afford that— but definitely high enough up that she didn't have to worry about traffic noise and more than one neighbor.

As soon as she stepped into the entryway of her condo some invisible tension left her spine. She loved the openness and the light from the wall of windows. Kicking her heels to the side, she dropped her bag to the tan marble floor and headed into the kitchen. There was a glass sitting on the counter she'd used this morning. Holding it to the dispenser in the fridge she waited for it to fill with water, then drank the thing down straight. Then she headed to the bathroom to change.

As she placed the blue suit onto a hanger for dry cleaning, she thought about what to have for dinner. The restaurant downstairs was superb and they would be willing to cook her anything she'd like, one of the perks of being a Waterford resident. On this cold, rainy day she was kind of just in the mood for soup and a sandwich, maybe.

Andromeda found a comfortable shirt and a pair of fleece pants to put on, then a loose sweater to go over top of everything. Yeah, now she was warm. Slipping her feet into her fuzzy slippers she padded out of the closet.

She ordered her food before picking up her laptop. Once she lost herself in the information it was hard to pull her mind back out. At least this way she could work a little, have a break, then work some more.

Settling onto the overstuffed couch in her living room, her favorite place to hang, she closed the vertical blinds over the rain-shrouded window. She glanced down from the height to the street below, but it was getting foggy. The

Scioto River, just a few hundred yards away, was warmer than the outside air apparently and sending up fog. It was a beautiful scene.

As she sank into her couch and pulled the laptop to her, she tried to think about every possible contingency she could imagine. If she had her preference, she would put both remaining witnesses under protective custody, but she doubted her boss would approve that kind of expense. Yes, this was a felony criminal case but there was only so far you could go with a budget as tight as theirs.

Andromeda pulled up the al Fareq file. His dark, vacant eyes had sent chills through her for months. It had only been in the past few weeks, as the trial date neared, that she'd finally started seeing the light at the end of the tunnel. Al Fareq would be convicted. She had no doubts about it. As long as she could get everyone into the courtroom.

CHAPTER 3

FOR SOME REASON he thought she'd be harder to find. Parker looked up the glass and concrete expanse of her condominium complex. It stretched at least thirty floors into the air and looked to be impenetrable. Parker knew that that was deceptive. Every building had a way in.

He shifted in the seat of the rental truck, trying to ease the pain in his right thigh. When it was cold and rainy like this it seemed to settle into the metal in his leg, chilling him from the inside out. He had two plates, a rod, and eight screws holding the upper leg together and it always caused him aggravation. The smaller plate in his left leg, not so much. The left ankle was a little weaker than the right and if anything let him down, it would be that ankle. It had sent him back to the doctor time after time and if he continued to have issues he was just going to have the bones fused permanently. Maybe then he'd at least be able to get around easier. Less pain would be a plus too.

Yeah, he thought that, but when it came time to actually admit himself to the hospital he doubted he could do it. Too many nightmares there. He would deal with the pain.

A late model BMW passed him and pulled into the underground parking garage. Parker picked up his binoculars. They had a nice security set-up here. The driver's side window stayed up, so he assumed there was some kind of scanner for the car, or a high-def camera to read a pass. Something like that. It was all very contained. The one way, metal gate went up and the car pulled in, brake lights shining.

Parker glanced at the parking loop at the front of the tower. There was a valet stand there doing a pretty brisk business, probably for the high-end restaurant on the back side of the first floor. There was a brass sign tucked at one corner of the building with a chef's name on it he didn't recognize, but that didn't mean anything. He was used to burgers and take-out.

Andromeda had pulled in earlier in her blacked-out Range Rover. The glass had been tinted but it had been enough for him to see her face. She hadn't been smiling. She'd looked... distracted, or something. Definitely hadn't been watching her surroundings.

Seeing her again brought back a whole slew of emotions. Anger and disillusionment, need and at the bottom of it all, heartbreak. The two of them had been something special.

Parker watched the front of the condo for a couple of hours before he pulled away from the building to park a block away. Then he walked back toward the condo. If he could scout out the surveillance they had on the building he'd have a better idea of where he stood.

It wasn't as hard as he'd feared. Within just a few minutes he found a way in through the delivery door in the back of the restaurant, propped open for the smokers to get out then back in easily. Parking himself under a dripping tree, he staked out the back, watching for a chance to slip in. It didn't take long. One of the waiters propped the door with a rock, smoked two cigarettes then let himself back into the building, leaving the rock in the prop position.

As Parker circled the building he wondered how many other security issues there were.

Two more. One was an unlocked side door into the restaurant and the second was a faulty camera, looking at that door. Overall the entire set-up was well thought out and executed, but for human error. Mentally, he marked the spots in his mind and circled around, heading back toward his truck. His toes were frozen and his left leg numb. When it thawed out it was going to be damn painful.

Back in his truck, he started swiping through screens on his smart phone he found the app that his current boss at Lost and Found had created. It was a simple tracking app. All you needed was the serial number on the transponder box and you could look it up on the GPS. It was ingenious, actually, and Palmer deserved to be proud of what he'd created.

When he'd walked through the Prosecutor's Office parking garage earlier, it had be surprisingly easy to set the box into the bumper of Andromeda's vehicle. As he looked the location up now and saw the steady little red target, he prayed she didn't have another vehicle. Or that she'd taken a cab somewhere, which she'd been known to do.

Parker poked at the menu icon in the top right-hand corner and set an alarm. If her car moved more than fifty feet he would be notified. Tipping his head back against the seat, he closed his eyes. In his rush to get here, he'd lost out on some sleep.

WHEN THE TEXT alarm on Andromeda's cell-phone went off at oh dark thirty, she had a premonition that it was going to be a bad day. Mike Maddox, her boss, wanted her to call him immediately.

"Cutting to the chase here," he told her quickly. "Your cop witness was just mowed down as he was walking to his cruiser in front of the police station. They think he'll be okay but he has a severe concussion, contusions and a broken shoulder. It was a late model sedan that hit him. One of the other cops got a partial plate so we're running it. If we find anything I'll let you know."

"This has to be the al Fareq case," Andromeda said quickly. "This is the third compromised witness. I need him under protection. I can't afford to lose any more people."

"I am aware," Mike told her calmly. "I've already got a call in for extra-duty officers. He'll be under twenty-four hour guard till next Wednesday. Where is your other guy?"

Andromeda sighed. "He's not far from here in German Village. I have to go get him before court. I think of any of them he'll be the safest because he's so far off the grid."

Zane Mackenzie was a mountain of a man with a dark auburn beard and arms that went on for miles. Quiet and observant, he'd become her prime witness. It also didn't hurt that he was a former Green Beret, retired after an injury. He'd mentally recorded details about the suspect that had basically given Andromeda her whole case.

Mac was a recluse, though, more comfortable with his books than dealing with the public. He liked to hang around East Whittier in the German Village neighborhood. There were several coffee and books shops around there. Though he'd agreed to be a witness in the criminal case, he wanted to fly under the radar as much as possible. He was not going to appreciate what was going on. He definitely would not appreciate being hauled in to be placed under protective custody.

Andromeda sat up in bed, the sheets falling around her. There was so much that she needed to do. "I'll be in at the office within the hour."

"I'll be there."

Andromeda bolted through her shower and got dressed. It was Saturday so she passed on the skirt suits and drew a pair of black pants from a hanger. Then a heavier maroon sweater. She had a pair of Bos and Company rain boots that would match the outfit fine and keep her feet dry. Last night they'd been damp, even though she'd been inside most of the day.

Letting the towel fall from her hair she started the moussing and styling process. Then she grabbed up her blow dryer. The short dark hair was styled within two minutes and she couldn't imagine what she'd done when her hair had been down to her waist. The *years* she'd wasted messing with it.

She packed her laptop into her bag and grabbed her coat from the hall closet, slipping it on. She would *not* get as chilled today as she had yesterday.

Charles was on duty this morning. She gave the monitor a wave as she headed down on the elevator, but wasn't in the mood to talk much. Instead she caught up on a few emails on her phone. Her head was down as she exited the elevator and she wasn't prepared when someone shoved into her. Clutching her phone in her hand she dropped it into her pocket as she looked up, ready to rip into someone. Andromeda had a split second to connect to a pair of dark eyes and a smiling face before she was instinctively jumping back from a vicious knife swing.

Her computer bag flopped against her hip and she put a

hand on it to protect the laptop, panting in shock. Andromeda knew her mouth was hanging open, but she couldn't seem to get a firm grasp on what was going on. The dark-eyed woman in the black hijab lunged at her again, barely missing Andromeda's stomach with the glittering blade.

Andromeda kicked at the woman's hand, but she held onto the knife, swinging around and slashing backwards. That one caught in her coat and Andromeda staggered back. Her back slammed into the concrete wall and the woman was on her, knife held overhead to plunge down. Gasping, Andromeda held her left arm up to protect her head and felt a scalding burn down her forearm, even through the leather of the coat. That was terrifying, and motivating. Balling her right fist, she plowed it toward the woman's face, but missed. Instead she grabbed the fabric of the hijab and pulled.

Her attacker screamed and fell away but Andromeda knew not to let her regain the advantage. Pushing away from the wall she balled her fist to punch her again, but her arm was grabbed before she could make contact. A much stronger force jerked her away and spun her to the concrete. She landed on her ass hard. A few yards away at the elevator doors a man in a knit cap was helping the woman up. They both turned to look at her. Scrambling to her feet Andromeda bolted for her vehicle. She knew the keys were in her pocket and if she could make it there she would be safe.

The boots weren't the best thing to run in but she made them work, her long legs eating up the ground. All those fucking hours at the gym were finally paying off. The car door unlocked as soon as she touched the handle and she lurched inside, jabbing at the button to start it. As soon as it caught she jerked the gear shift into drive. Something thumped against the hood and she looked up to see the woman standing in front of her vehicle with her arms spread, a maniacal smile twisting her lips. Was she trying to die?

The man slammed something black and hard against her driver's side window and Andromeda winced. Had that been a gun? If he broke the glass he'd be able to grab her. Pushing her foot onto the gas pedal she drove out of the spot. The woman in the hijab fell to the side, screaming unintelligible things at her, but she seemed to be okay. The man chased after her for several yards before she lost sight of him as she turned a corner. She paused for the sensor to read her vehicle to open the gate, but when she saw that man running up behind her she panicked. Flooring it, she rammed through the metal gate barring the exit.

Outside, there was another melee going on that she couldn't make sense of. It looked like several men, all with middle-eastern coloring like the two that had just attacked her, had piled onto one big Caucasian male. They had him on the ground and were pounding the hell out of him, it looked like.

Andromeda was torn. Had the man seen something and been trying to help her? Or was he just in the wrong place at the wrong time?

Her tires barked on the pavement as she turned onto the street and started away. Then she glanced into the rearview mirror.

One of the middle-eastern men held a gun out toward the man on the ground, then the man on the ground brought one out as well. The attackers scattered away when it appeared they were going to be in the middle of a firefight. Time stilled, and she stomped on the brakes. Desperate to derail what was about to happen, she blew her horn and slammed the vehicle into reverse.

The transmission whined as she floored the Range Rover into a controlled back up, targeting the standing man with the gun. He didn't even glance up at the car barreling down on him until it was almost too late. At the last possible moment, he glanced up. Even as he started to lunge away, the gun went off. Then a second gun went off. Even inside the vehicle she could hear the report of the weapons.

Andromeda jerked the wheel to the side, parking the Range Rover between the attackers and the man on the ground. She looked down at him, screaming for him to get up and get in. But some piece of her consciousness realized that she'd stepped into a time warp. She recognized the man like she'd spoken to him just yesterday, though it had been years. Parker Quinn lay on the ground, squinting in pain, black gun in hand.

Parker Quinn? Seriously? What the ever loving fuck was going on?

He scrambled to his feet, though it seemed like it took him a very long time. Was he in pain? Even as he lunged into the rear seat, she was already flooring the vehicle. It took him a moment to get all the way into the seat and close the door, but she didn't dare slow down to let him get situated. She stared at him in the rearview mirror though. Even as she drove like the devil was on her ass, she stared at her former lover in the back seat.

"Turn here," he snapped. "Right. Right."

Andromeda slammed on the brakes and cranked the wheel.

"Stop beside that gray pickup."

She followed the line of Parker's finger and stopped beside a non-descript Chevy truck. Tumbling out of her vehicle he keyed a remote for the gray pickup and reached inside. He pulled out a big tan duffel, shut the door, locked it and got back into her vehicle, this time in the front seat.

"Go!"

Andromeda floored it, terrified that any minute now she would see a car in pursuit.

For some reason she turned away from the prosecutor's office and headed toward High Street. There was plenty of traffic there and plenty of places to pull over and take a breath.

Parker was talking to her but there was a ringing in her ears that deafened her. She could see his hard lips moving but couldn't hear his beautiful voice.

Andromeda pulled into a Wendy's and parked her car, then let her head sag to the steering wheel as she caught her breath. Her heart was pounding out of her chest as she thought about what she'd just done. Yes, she'd been attacked but she had also attacked someone, struck her with a motor vehicle, committed criminal damage against her condo company, and committed a vehicular assault. Her brain shorted out and she knew she had to call her boss. And the condo company. How the hell had she gotten in this mess?

God, she needed to call Charles just to give him a heads up. Surely by now he'd called the cops? There were security cameras all over that building.

Andromeda scrambled in her pocket for her phone, but she remembered Parker. Twisting in her seat she looked at him.

Leaning against the door he scanned the area constantly, black gun still in hand. His big body was dressed in black from head to toe, but she didn't need bare skin to remember what he looked like. Stacked with muscle from his neck down, he was— and always had been— one of the most attractive men she'd ever been in the presence of. His deep-set gunmetal gray eyes regarded her thoughtfully as she caught her breath. "You okay?"

Andromeda blinked, wondering what crazy hell she'd managed to drop into. She nodded, but wasn't sure she was telling him the truth.

Parker grinned at her, his hard, angular face softening as he slicked his sweaty hair back with a hand. It was normally a buttery dirty blond, but right now, dark with sweat, it was almost a walnut color. "You kicked some ass back there."

Suddenly she was twenty-five years old and blushing from a compliment by a good looking guy in a bar. How trite was it that she met him when they were both out with friends? She hadn't really been looking for anything in particular, maybe just some attention and a good time. Unfortunately, the attention was easy to get— the good time, not so much.

She and two of her girlfriends had been leaning over a pool table, playing haphazardly. They hadn't actually been getting a lot of balls into pockets, but they had been playing. Andromeda had looked up and there had been a man staring at her. This man. He'd been a newly minted Navy SEAL, in Boston for some super-secret training. Within just a few minutes he'd managed to work his way close to the table. He'd teased her into playing a game with him and it had been daring and frightening and thrilling. Parker Quinn made her feel things that she'd never felt before and she'd gotten high just from being close to him.

Most of the guys she went to law school with had more money than brains, so to find someone that wasn't ruled by what his daddy wanted or what society expected was a scintillating change. And he was just young and brash enough to walk into a college bar and turn the girls on their heads.

There was a realness to him that had called to her.

And now, years later with so much mileage between them, he still called to her. Her eyes drank him in.

"What the hell are you doing here?"

"I'm protecting you," he told her.

Andromeda barked out a laugh. "Okay, I must have missed that part. Are you serious?"

Parker scanned the area, looking as dangerous as she knew him to be. "Hey, they were all heading in toward you and I sidetracked most of them."

One finger brushed at the blood at the corner of his mouth and she felt a little bad. He *had* been there.

"I can't believe what just happened."

"Well, we need to get you the hell out of here. It's not safe for you to be here."

Reaching into her center console she brought out a pack of baby wipes and plucked several from the package. "Look at me," she told him.

He turned his head to her and she started wiping blood away. Something seemed off about his face, but she couldn't tell what exactly. She looked at him, turning his head this way and that. There were some faint lines around his right eye.

"It's not going to even out," he told her finally. "I've had some damage to my right eye socket, so things look a little off."

Abruptly she pulled her hands away. "Oh, I am so sorry! I thought you had swelling but I couldn't see where."

"Don't worry about it. It's been a while. We need to get out of here," he reminded her.

Andromeda nodded. "I think you're right. I need to call my boss and tell him what happened."

As she drew the phone up, Parker pushed her hand

down. "I think we need to get you out of Dodge first. If you stay, you're going to have to do a police report and all that shit. Let's get you out of town and then you can call. Once he understands it was for your safety it'll all work out."

Andromeda gave him a look out of the corner of her eyes. "Why are you here, Parker? And why are you trying to get me out of town?"

He grinned and shook his head slowly. "I knew you'd question everything. Let's just say that there are interests invested in keeping you alive. And they want these terrorists you're trying to convict as gone as you do. I'm here to make sure you succeed. But we have to leave. Your apartment is compromised."

Andromeda scowled and rested her head back on her hands. What a clusterfuck. She shook her head. "I don't have any clothes or anything with me. I can't just leave."

He frowned at her and gave her a strange look.

"Sure, you can. You just drive away. Anything we need we can get on the road."

She blinked, shocked at the ease with which he said that. "No, I am an officer of the court. I have a responsibility to report what happened and file charges if anyone has been apprehended."

Parker shook his head, resigned. "Fine. Call your boss, but don't tell him where you are."

Andromeda paged through to Mike's number and pressed the phone, then the speaker button. He answered on the first ring.

"What the fuck is going on, Andromeda? What happened at your condo?"

"I was attacked. First by a woman as I got off the elevator, then by a man that was with her. I made it to my car and had to drive through the gate to get out of the parking garage. Outside, there was a ..." she hesitated, glancing at Parker in the seat beside her. "A friend that had been attacked as well by four other men. All of the men looked to be of Middle Eastern descent and they were armed."

"Where are you now?" he demanded.

Andromeda winced. "I'm at a Wendy's debating what to do. As crazy as it sounds I'm going to go ahead and get Mac and get out of town for a few days. They're trying to get rid of us all, Mike."

"Andromeda, if Mozi doesn't accept the plea agreement you have trial in five days. Is it really the best time to be taking off?"

"Her life is in danger," Parker growled. "She's leaving town for at least four days."

"Who the hell is this?" Mike demanded.

"Parker Quinn, US Navy SEAL, retired. Andromeda could have been killed today. If I hadn't been there she definitely would have come to harm, at the very least, or been kidnapped. While she's gone, why don't you find out who the hell is after her. You've had months to figure out what was going on. Any lay person can see there's a terror cell in your city."

"And we're doing everything we can about that, buddy," Mike snapped.

"Well, while you guys throw paper at the terrorists to try to get them to be good, I'll be throwing bullets at them if they come near us. Got that?"

Silence stretched on the other end of the line. "Fine. Go get your witness, Andromeda. Are you ready for trial?"

"As ready as I can be, yes. I have my laptop with me so I can work remotely."

"You do that. And Andromeda?"

"Yes?"

"You better damn well keep me updated."

And he hung up.

Andromeda sagged in her seat, wondering what in the hell she'd gotten herself into. Yes, she was battling crime and getting danger off the streets, but it seemed never ending. And the deeper she went the more dangerous her life seemed to become.

Her eyes filled with tears and she had to force them back. The morning had been horrendous. In all of her thirty-three years, she'd never been attacked like that in her life. She'd never really even been punched or hit. And she certainly had never had someone actually try to take her life.

A weight settled onto her back. Parker's broad hand, apparently, because it began rubbing back and forth, over her coat. Her skin came to life, sending chills through her.

"Where did you come from?" she asked faintly.

"Colorado," he snorted. "But my old commander called me up and told me I needed to be here. I'm glad he did. Otherwise you would probably be dead."

Yes, she probably would be, and that pissed her off. What right did this family have to try to kill her?

Sitting up in her seat, Andromeda wiped her cheeks. "Yes, I think you're right. Okay, what do we need to do?"

"We need to get the fuck out of here before some random passerby just happens to know someone looking for you."

Andromeda looked out the windshield to see a bedraggled homeless man looking right at them. She slammed the car into reverse and turned right out of the parking lot.

"We have to find Mac," she said decisively.

CHAPTER 4

PARKER SHIFTED IN THE SEAT, already feeling cramped. Reaching down for the seat controls, he slid his back as far as it would go. Better, but still not great.

They merged into traffic at a stoplight and Andromeda glanced around nervously. He wanted to try to calm her fears, but it was probably best that she stay sharp. Holstering his Heckler Koch Mk 23, he sat back in the seat and tried to find a more comfortable position for his legs.

"How far away is this guy?"

Andromeda glanced at him with a wince. "It depends upon where he is."

"What?"

She shrugged, looking pale in her dark coat. "He's a bit of a wanderer. He doesn't always stay in one place, but German Village is where he lives. We set a time to meet next week but I'm early."

She took two more turns before she started to slow down. Parker looked around.

This area had a lot of character. History was written upon every brick building and landscaped yard. Even the streets were brick. It had been a long time since he'd been in such a well-cared for area. It was obvious there was a strong sense of civic pride here.

Andromeda pulled up in front of a book store and coasted past. There were several wrought iron benches around, but they were all empty.

"We may not see him," she murmured. "It's early yet. Nothing is open. He likes to sit on the benches and read. I've never seen a man read like he does."

She merged back into traffic and drove a few blocks, then turned left. A giant park opened up beside them. The rain had held off today, so joggers and dog walkers used the paths. It was a nice, crisp fall morning.

Lips pursed, Andromeda drove along the perimeter of the park, eyes darting here and there. When they completed the circle, she pulled into a parking spot. "I know he likes to come here to read. It's his favorite place. Do you want to hang out a few minutes or come back?"

Parker could tell she was distraught and needed a break. He scanned the area. It seemed quiet enough, in a weird way. There were people out, but the Range Rover fit in like she lived here. "I think we'll be okay for a bit."

Andromeda turned the ignition off and melted into the seat. She looked drawn and worried, but still incredibly beautiful.

Parker had never seen anything like her. Tall and athletic, she must be an imposing figure in the courtroom. But her face was ethereal. She had the finest pored skin he'd ever seen, smooth as porcelain. The wings of her brows were strong and delicate. And her eyes... her eyes. A man could lose himself for years in the depths of her golden topaz eyes. They were so unique. He'd seen men and women both do double takes when they talked to her.

High cheekbones and a strong chin gave her the perfect oval face. Her lips gave her a sensuality to balance out her stark bone structure. Her dark hair had been cut almost boyishly short. If she'd been trying to reduce her femininity by cutting off her long, almost-black hair it hadn't worked. The short cut was a little longer in front and gave her a pixie-ish cuteness that she would probably smack him for if he ever told her.

He glanced down her body, wishing that she wasn't wearing the bulky coat. She'd had one of the most beautiful bodies he'd ever seen. It had been many years since he'd seen her but he assumed her curves were still there. Yesterday she'd worn that rain jacket, camouflaging all her good parts.

But her looks were such a small part of who she was. When he'd met her in a bar years ago she'd been letting off steam after taking some big lawyer test in school and she'd been exuberant, her eyes glowing with an inner strength he'd never seen in another woman. She was well on her path to being a lawyer and she loved everything about her profession.

Parker was just as passionate about being a SEAL. He lived and breathed weapons and tactics and strategy. He took every training they offered; it was why he was in Boston. It had been refreshing to find someone as invested in their career as he'd been. Unfortunately, his career had burned out sooner than he'd expected. Hers seemed to still be going strong.

Andromeda glanced at him, then down at her hands. "I was pretty shocked to see you. You look good, Parker. Really good. What have you been doing?"

He sighed, knowing that this would come up at some time. And she was being kind about his looks. He hadn't been that good looking guy for a long time. "Well, I was with the SEALs for several years, before I got... injured. Then they politely kicked me out the door."

She frowned. "Seriously? Why would they do that?"

Parker shrugged, looking out the window. Anxiety began to creep into his bones. "Mind of I crack this window?"

He pressed the button to roll the window down a couple of inches, inhaling the moist air.

"Don't worry about it," she said eventually. "You don't have to tell me."

Parker wanted to tell her, kind of. He could tell by the sound of her voice that she was a little hurt. But it was too damned soon to get into something so heavy. They'd been together less than an hour and he didn't know which way this situation was going to go. Depending upon how things went he could be here a day or two weeks, and he didn't plan on engaging in anything with her. Besides, after all this time there was a chance she was already attached to someone. No, there was no ring on her finger, but that didn't necessarily mean anything. Andromeda was a busy lawyer. Maybe she just didn't have time for attachments.

Parker couldn't say anything. He'd never gotten involved with anyone either. At least, not after Andromeda. Yes, there'd been more than his fair share of hookups, but no one he could tolerate for more than a few hours. Definitely no one that he'd consider giving up his lifestyle for.

"How are your mom and dad?" she asked.

Parker gave her a tight smile, appreciating the subject change. "They're fine. Still doing their thing in Pennsylvania. They've got a timeshare now in Hawaii they've been jetting back and forth to. It's a nice diversion for them and every time they go over they stay longer. I expect them to tell me any time they're moving over permanently."

"That's a long way from ... Colorado, was it you said?"

Parker glanced at her quickly. Andromeda remembered every detail. "Yes. Denver."

She cleared her throat. "Are you married, or do you have kids or anything?"

Parker blinked at the directness of the question. "Um, no, to both. You?"

For some reason her cheeks turned a little pink and she shook her head. "Nope. Always the bridesmaid, never the bride."

Frowning, Parker studied her expression. That sounded a little bitter. "I'm sorry."

"Don't worry about it," she said quickly. "It's not your fault."

"How are your parents," he asked, desperate for a topic.

"They're fine. They moved up New Hampshire to be near my sister and her kids. She has three now."

Parker blinked. "Damn. She got busy, didn't she? Was she even married when we were together?"

Andy shook her head, a small smile on her lips. "No. She and Ben fell hard and fast."

Clamping her lips shut she looked out the window, her thumbnails running over top of each other repeatedly. Why did Parker feel like he needed to be on the defensive?

"Andy, what's wrong?"

The familiar shortening of her name slipped off his tongue without thought. Making a face she glanced at him.

"Not very many people call me Andy." She laughed throatily. "It sounds strange coming from you. I haven't been *that* Andy for years."

"You'll always be Andy to me."

She stared at him for a long moment and opened her mouth to say something, then decided better of it. She turned back to the driver's side window.

Parker felt like he was walking on eggshells. Their relationship had been hot and fiery, and ended just as abruptly. They'd both been at fault and he thought he may have been further along in the relationship than she'd been.

"There he is," she gasped.

Parker followed the line of her finger. There was a big man sitting on a bench on the far side of the park. Even from this far away he could see how big the man was. He held a leather bound book in his massive hands and was flipping through pages, obviously looking for his spot. His head was down and he wore a fedora hat, but Parker could still see the mass of reddish-brown hair springing from beneath was sprinkled with gray. He had a beard several inches long and the same vibrant hue as his hair, other than the streak of gray on his chin. The man wore some type of vest with multiple pockets bulging with paraphernalia, with a brick red plaid shirt beneath. Tan pants with yet more pockets finished off his ensemble, and a pair of well-worn loafers.

"That's your eyewitness? He looks like a nutty professor."

Andromeda laughed. "You are more right than you know."

She stepped out of the vehicle and started across the park to the man. Parker cursed, wishing she'd driven closer to the bench where he sat. This was going to fuck with his legs. He prayed the ground was more level than it appeared.

The big man looked up as Andromeda approached him and a cautious, disappointed look slid over his face. "Ms. Pierce."

"Hello, Mac." She reached out and shook his hand. "I'm

so sorry to bother you, but can I talk to you a moment?"

The big man motioned at the expanse of bench beside him. He took up a lot of room himself, but there was enough for Andromeda's slim form. Parker paused a few yards away and scanned the area. He would let Andromeda work out the details with Mac.

Mac was younger than he seemed from a distance, maybe in his mid-forties, and though he was big, Parker didn't believe it was fat. He had a quiet, strong disposition about him, and his blue eyes were sharp as they scanned Andromeda's scuffed clothing, as well as Parker's.

Traffic was beginning to pick up and he felt very exposed. His legs were aching from fighting and he had a scrape down his right shin. His left elbow was throbbing and his knuckles were busted, but he was ready to go again if he needed to.

Andromeda murmured softly behind him, filling Mac in on what was going on. His answering bass rumble was unintelligible.

A jogger swung around Parker, her dark ponytail swinging. A man and his dog followed along behind, the dog passing close enough to Parker to strain against the leash in friendliness.

A car passed by, the sound of the tires on the brick streets making an odd vibration sound. It had been years since he'd seen brick streets anywhere.

Andromeda called his name and he turned, then stepped toward them. Mac looked him up and down, considering, and he eventually held out a ham-sized hand. Parker shook the hand without hesitation. "Mr. Mackenzie. It's a pleasure to meet you."

Mac frowned as if testing his words, then drew his hand back. He didn't respond to Parker's pleasantry, but Parker didn't blame him. They'd kind of just fucked up his reading time.

Without saying anything more Parker turned to survey the area. A few more people had entered the park. The young woman with the stroller wasn't an issue, but another jogger, male, had entered the property, as well as a couple of teenagers. One had his head down, typing into a phone. The other was running commentary into his ear, like he was telling him what to write. The whisperer glanced up and his gaze connected with Parker's.

Parker's Spidey senses went on alert and he looked away, but kept the two kids in his peripheral vision. They were a hundred yards away, but that space could be closed quickly. He glanced over his shoulder at Andromeda. "We need to get out of here."

She glanced around, panic in her eyes, but he shook his head. "Nothing specific, we just need to get off the street."

He met Mac's eyes and the other man seemed to get a sense of what Parker was feeling, because he pushed up off the bench. "Let's sit in your car, Ms. Pierce."

They started walking back toward the car, taking the direct route over the grass rather than the twisting paved sidewalk. As soon as they started to move the teenagers turned to look at them, and Parker knew he'd been right. Something was up. Those kids had probably just broadcast their location to whomever was after them.

Putting himself between the kids and Andromeda, he forced his legs into a light jog, tugging her along behind him. One of the kids gave a shout and the race was on. In spite of the pain in his leg he ran as fast as he could, towing her along behind.

"Mac, no," Andromeda yelled.

Parker glanced back to see Mac facing off with the two

kids. There was a fixed blade knife in his right hand and he looked like he knew how to use it. Shoving Andromeda toward the vehicle he turned toward Mac. "Get the car, Andy. I'll protect Mac."

There were two pops and Parker looked around wildly, trying to see where they'd come from. His own gun was in his hand, but he didn't want to fire until he could actually see a target. There were too many innocent bystanders around.

The shots hadn't been from the kids. His eyes scanned over the pond to the copse of trees. There. Had he seen a flash of movement between the trees? They were so fucking exposed here. But it also worked to their advantage. There weren't a lot of places people could hide.

The dirt and grass in front of him exploded where two more gunshots struck. He gripped Mac's arm and tugged on it, pulling him back. On the far side of the park Andy's Range Rover started, the engine revving.

The teenagers pelted into a run toward them, heedless of who was watching. Parker saw the flash of black-bladed knives in their hands.

Mac was a big man, but he could still move when he needed to. Parker heard a scream and a crash and looked back to see Andy's black vehicle barreling toward them across the grass. The shooter must have sensed that they were going to lose their advantage because the bullets started flying in earnest then and even suppressed as they were, it still made noise. Innocent bystanders ran away, and those that were still in the park and heading toward them clarified their position as enemies. Parker opened fire without further hesitation.

One of the teens fell as Parker winged him in the shoulder. The second he shot in the knee. But while he'd slowed to focus his target, the shooter across the pond had done the same. Parker felt himself get shot. It felt like getting hit by a Mack truck in the right side of his body. Suddenly he was down and eating dirt. He gave himself the briefest second to breathe, then pushed himself to his hands and knees. He had to get moving again. But his bad legs failed him. He didn't have the range of motion anymore to just lunge to his feet. Normally, he braced his body against something— a chair or a counter— to get to his feet. But those things weren't available.

Luckily, a red haired mountain of a man was. Mac had returned for him. Just as Parker was lifted to his feet, Andy slammed the car to a stop beside them, grass and dirt churning.

Parker had a glimpse of her pale, terrified face just before Mac helped him into the back seat of the vehicle. Parker groaned as he lurched across to the other side and lowered the window. He'd kept hold of his weapon, but he could not spot a target. Whoever had been shooting at him from the trees had apparently moved. Or they were hunkered down and reloading.

"You need to get us the fuck out of here, Andy."

Without a word, she *floored* it. The wheels spun in the soft grass, then caught hold and launched them across the space. As they reached the other side of the park the gunfire started again. Parker heard a thunk against the rear of the vehicle then they were going airborne. They landed hard and he heard the hum of brick streets beneath the tires. Scanning the area behind them he watched for signs of pursuit, but Andy had apparently slipped them again.

"Make us disappear, Andy. Get us into traffic."

She did exactly that. Within just a few minutes they were merging onto I70 eastbound and the morning rush hour. Any other time he'd have bitched about the bumper to bumper cars, but right now they served a purpose.

His adrenaline was beginning to equalize, though, allowing pain to creep in. His legs were throbbing, but it was a drop in the bucket compared to the blazing pain in his right side. He looked down at himself and he could tell he was bleeding pretty good. Parker pulled his shirt up and cringed at the sight of the bullet wound in his side. Reaching his hand around his torso, he felt to the back. Yup, there it was. The exit wound. It was close enough to his side, though, that he didn't think anything vital had been hit.

Parker looked for something to put pressure against the wound. There was a maroon towel on the floorboard and a small throw blanket on the seat. Reaching for the towel he folded it up into a length about a foot long and pressed it against the wound.

"Did we kill a kid back there?"

Andy's frantic golden eyes met his in the rearview mirror. He shook his head. "Nope. I shot one in the leg and the other in the shoulder. They'll both live to terrorize again."

She seemed to completely miss the dry humor. "I can't believe this is going on. How the hell did my life go to hell so quickly? How do we get out of this?"

She seemed to be asking him an actual question. Parker shrugged. "I think we disappear for a few days. If we play it right they'll never even notice we left. They know court is in a few days so they won't expect us to leave."

"So, you think it's connected to the al Fareq case?" She shook her head. "Of course it is, stupid."

She had a death grip on the steering wheel, her eyes staring ahead dazedly.

"Andy, you need to watch your speed and be aware of what is around you. I don't think we were followed but it's hard to tell in this traffic. We need to come up with a place to stay."

She nodded, her foot easing off the gas pedal. She merged into the right-hand lane and set the cruise control, then, finally, some of the tension went out of her shoulders.

"I have an idea on where we can go. It's a few hours away but I know of a cabin in West Virginia."

"West Virginia," Mac asked incredulously. "I can't go to West Virginia."

"Why not? It's out of their reach."

"I have obligations," he said quickly. "Things I can't leave alone for several days."

"I think your obligations will wait on you. Are they really more important than your life?"

Mac looked out the side window. He looked fine, considering what he'd just been through. His hat still perched on his fuzzy hair and his clothes were no more ruffled than when he'd sat on the bench. Pulling a phone from his pocket he texted someone, then sat brooding.

How had Parker ended up with the shitty end of the stick today? Hadn't he had enough pain in his life? Even as he thought it a spasm of pain made him hunch into himself. Breathing hard, he tried to concentrate on something else, but it was hard.

Gravity was getting harder to fight.

"You should call your boss, Andy, and fill him in on what just happened. He's going to have to send a cleaning crew out."

Nodding she reached for her phone but he was too far gone to care. He let his eyes drift closed as he slid down in the seat.

CHAPTER 5

IT WASN'T until Andromeda hung up from Mike that she realized Parker wasn't running his usual constant commentary. She glanced back at him. He looked to be ass out asleep. Could he really be that unconcerned?

She looked back at the interstate, a little put out. How had she become the one everyone was relying upon?

"Is he okay?" She asked Mac.

The older man craned his head around to look at Parker. "I suppose so. Want me to wake him up?"

"No," she said slowly. Then she reconsidered. "Yes, wake him please."

Mac turned in his seat and prodded at Parker. "Hey, boy. You picked a damn fool time to sleep."

Parker turned his head but didn't rouse. Andromeda thought she heard him murmur something but couldn't make it out. Parker used to be a really light sleeper. That prodding should have woken him up easily.

"There's an exit coming up and I need gas anyway."

Mac turned back in his seat and looked ahead at the large truck stop looming at the side of the interstate. "We might go ahead and get some snacks and stuff too. Do you know *where* in West Virginia we're going?"

Andromeda nodded but didn't tell him where. Years ago, she'd represented a woman in a brutal rape and assault case. She'd gotten a conviction against the hospital administration and a hefty settlement because of their negligence. The woman, Rosalind White, had gained Andromeda's respect and they'd become good friends. Rosalind lived in Georgia now, but she had a cabin in the woods of West Virginia. They'd met there several times over the years for little escape weekends, and Roz had told Andy she could use the cabin any time. So that was where they were headed.

Andromeda put her blinker on and swung off the ramp then into the gas station parking lot. Mac headed inside to stock up on what he needed. She used her card and inserted the nozzle to pump gas, then opened the passenger side door to check on Parker. His head had been resting against the door and he didn't respond as she reached out to touch his face.

"Parker!"

Now truly alarmed Andromeda tapped his cheeks. He blinked his eyes open but didn't seem to be focusing.

"Parker, what's wrong? Why weren't you answering?"

He blinked, his eyes clearing. "Andy? Why are you upside down?"

She grinned at him. "I'm not. You are. You're lying on the back seat of my car."

Parker craned his neck up to look and hissed in a breath, his hands going to his abdomen. Andromeda focused on the area and realized that it was wet. *Was that blood?*

Reaching out she pulled the black t-shirt away from his abdomen. The towel that she used for the inside of her windows was wrapped around his middle and she could tell it was soaked as well. Had he been shot and they just hadn't noticed it?

The gas nozzle clicked off and she looked around at the crowded pumps. This wasn't the place to check out his gunshot wound, but they needed to. Maybe she could drive around back or over to one of the corners where it was less crowded.

Mac opened the other rear door and looked through the vehicle at her.

"I think Parker's been shot," she told him quietly.

Mac's eyes widened comically and he stilled, then lurched into action. "Finish up with the gas. We need to get somewhere where we can check him out. There are too many people around here."

She did as she was told, buttoning things up as quickly as she could. She shut the rear door carefully, making sure not to bang his head. Then she hopped in the driver's seat and pulled away from the pumps. They circled the gas station. On the backside of the building, near the giant grease traps, the parking lot was completely deserted. Probably because it stank so bad. Mac got out as soon as she parked and opened the back door. Andromeda got up onto her knees between the front seats and leaned into the back, again lifting Parker's shirt. Then, with Mac nodding her on, she peeled away the towel. There was an angry hole, so red it was black, beneath the padding and as soon as she pulled the terrycloth away from his body fresh blood welled and began to run down his side.

"Oh, fuck," she breathed.

Even Mac looked a little rattled. "Hold that cloth on the wound. I'm going to go back into the gas station and see what kind of first aid kits they have. I'll get some bottled water and see what else they have we can use."

Andromeda nodded and pushed the towel against the wound. Parker groaned and rolled his head toward her. "S'okay, Andy. I know you're trying to hel' me. I might jus' close my eyes for a bit."

"You close your eyes, Parker. We're probably going to have to get you up in a few minutes, but we'll get you fixed up enough to travel, okay?"

He gave a single nod. "It went clear through. If you can get the bleeding stopped I would be... very appreciative."

She laughed weakly. "I'll do the best I can," she promised.

He reached up a hand to brush against her cheek. "You're so beautiful," he whispered. "I missed you." Then his eyes closed and his hand fell back to his side.

Andromeda fought not to cry. Somehow, she'd landed herself into his crazy situation and it was taking her a while to acclimate to everything going on. She was so far out of her depth it wasn't even funny. They should all be in protective custody right now. Mike had offered it when she'd called in earlier, but she'd declined. If they could just drop off the grid for a few days they would all be safe.

One of the things he'd told her to do was to live off cash. As soon as they got Parker patched up she was going to go clean up in the truck stop and get as much cash out of her account her bank would allow. They shouldn't need a great deal for three days, but she would still get out as much as possible. Before they got to the cabin she would stop at a grocery store. Then, when they got to the cabin they could decide what else they needed. Surely, those people wouldn't be able to follow them three hundred miles away. She'd never talked about the cabin or Rosalind to anyone.

Mac returned with two large first aid kits, half a dozen bottles of water and a bottle of peroxide. He also brought a package of maxipads. When he lifted the pink package out of the bag she lifted her brows at him. "They're great blood absorbers. I used to carry them in my own pack."

Oh. Okay.

They managed to get Parker out of the vehicle and on his feet. Mac held him up as Andromeda climbed into the back and laid the seats down, creating an expansive space in the back of the vehicle. She sighed at the sight of the ruined leather before she released the latch on the side, but there was no fixing it. Once everything was flat she helped Mac get Parker back into the vehicle, lying diagonally, then they climbed in beside him. Mac pulled the back hatch down over them for privacy but didn't let it latch.

It was difficult getting Parker's shirt over his head, but they managed, and she had to stop and stare for a moment, stunned.

Andromeda had no idea what had happened to Parker, but it really looked like he'd been tortured at some point in his career. Literally. Old white scars ran across most of his body. There was no rhyme or reason to them, just a conglomeration of scarred flesh. There were two spots on his upper chest that looked like gunshot wounds, but she didn't know enough about them to be sure. There were surgery scars on his left upper arm. She could see the small blemishes the stitches had left. The man still had the body of a SEAL, though, strong and lean. Tempting.

A breath expanded his broad chest and she realized he still looked good to her. Was it compassion, desperation or loneliness that made her want to reach out and stroke his poor skin? When she'd been with him he'd had the body of a Greek god. The muscles were all still there, but he no longer had the beautiful aesthetics.

Andromeda looked up at Mac. He'd been surveying all of the old wounds as well and his eyes had gone cold. But when she would have asked him what he thought he very deliberately shook his head.

Parker had passed out as soon as they laid him down again and he didn't make a sound as they began cleaning him up. Mac took the lead in this, but he handed her a pair of gloves from the first aid kit. "I might need some help."

And he did, when he needed to roll Parker up onto his side so that he could look at the bullet's exit wound. Andromeda had told him what Parker had said about the wound and that was exactly what they found. On the one hand she was really happy to know that the bullet was no longer in his body, but on the other hand the exit wound looked horrendous.

"I've seen worse," Mac assured her. "This looks bad but it's actually pretty clean. If I had suture material I'd put a few stitches in but for now, we'll just clean and pack it. I really don't think it hit anything vital."

He doused the area with water, patted him dry with a wad of paper towels and muttered something about infection. He layered three pads over the exit wound, then three more over the entrance wound, and wrapped Parker's entire lower torso in sticky athletic tape. It wasn't especially pretty but the bleeding had stopped completely. Covering him with the blanket, she and Mac left the back.

After they each stripped off their gloves and put them in the grocery sack for disposal, Mac reached out and squeezed her shoulder. "You did good. Thank you for not freaking out."

Andromeda gave a gasp of laughter and nodded. "No problem. I'm going to go clean up," she said.

They gathered everything bloody and put it into the plastic grocery sack, then Andromeda headed for the front of the truck stop. Mac would wait here with their patient while she went inside to get cleaned up and grab some snacks and cash.

Andromeda headed straight for the women's room to wash up and dispose of the bloody evidence. She washed her hands for a good ten minutes, until the icy temperature threatened to numb her hands completely. She stared into the glass over the sink, wondering how her life had gotten so out of control. Two days ago she'd been prepping for one of the biggest cases of her life. Now she was on the run for her life, literally. And that of her prime witness.

She needed to get her ass moving. Finishing up in the bathroom she walked out into the store, and to the ATM machine. Her bank allowed her to get out five hundred dollars. Not a great deal but it should be plenty for the few days they'd be gone. When she got back into the car she'd hide her card and rely only on cash.

She grabbed two bottles of water as well as two energy drinks. In the snack aisle she grabbed two bags of beef jerky as well as a couple of different bags of trail mix. From a rack with dried fruit so she grabbed a container of pineapple and another of peaches. Probably loaded with sugar but it might be what Parker needed when he woke up. Returning to the cooler she grabbed two bottles of Diet Pepsi, his favorite. Or, it had been his favorite years ago.

The chocolate at the cash register tempted her so she grabbed a few candy bars as well as two king sized bags of peanut M&Ms. Again, Parker's favorite from years ago. Not her own. Deliberately she grabbed a container of spearmint gum, and a Payday. That was more her speed.

She walked out of the truck stop with two bags of crap. When she got to the car she automatically looked into the back. Parker was laying as they'd left him, unconscious. She took off her coat, folded it up and propped his head on it, then turned back around and strapped in. "Okay. Let's get this done."

CHAPTER 6

MAC SIGHED as he looked out the window. No matter how much you tried to keep to yourself and mind your own business something always came along to change that.

When he'd seen the truck barreling along the streets that day all those months ago at the Columbus Art Fair, it was like some trained reflex had turned his record light on. After years of serving as a grunt in the Army, then later as a Green Beret, he'd had training upon training for exactly those types of incidents. Even years after he'd been discharged, that training had been so deeply ingrained that he probably couldn't have avoided everything that had happened.

It had been his choice to step forward though. That was how he'd screwed himself. After so many years of being screwed for being the good guy, when would he learn?

The police officer that had taken his statement had stared at him in shock as Mac had reeled off distances traveled and shots fired down to the second. He'd been turned over to the detective in charge very quickly after that. It probably wasn't usual for an eye witness to walk a crime scene and tell the detective where to place the evidence markers, but he had. And later, when everything had been measured and marked, every single one of Mac's details had been proven or verified.

As a witness he was solid gold, he knew that. And so did Andromeda. So all of this that they were going through would be worth it in the end if it would get this group of terrorists out of Columbus before more people were hurt.

The job didn't end just because he no longer wore the uniform.

He glanced into the back. The big SEAL hadn't moved, which was probably a good thing. They had very little holding him together at the moment. If he struggled he would rip everything open again and get it bleeding.

"Where are we going?" he asked eventually.

Andromeda looked at him for a moment before turning back to the interstate in front of her. "A friend of mine has a cabin down here and I've been there several times. It's off the grid and incredibly quiet."

He turned to look out at the running gray of the highway. "Okay."

She laughed a little. "No argument?"

He shook his head. "Nah. As long as we have some food and entertainment," he drew a book from one of his pockets, "we should be fine. Although you might think about trying to find Mr. Perfect back there some antibiotics and suture material."

She frowned. "I know. Just not sure where to get that stuff. The owner of the cabin is a former nurse. Maybe she'll have something there we can use."

Mac didn't say anything for a few minutes, preferring to watch the miles slide by. Then curiosity got the better of him. "Seems like you know Mr. Quinn personally."

Andromeda clasped both hands onto the steering wheel and leaned forward, obviously changing the position of her back to stretch muscles. "I used to," she said finally. "I haven't seen him for years but back when I was in law school we had a supernova affair."

She smiled as she remembered, the tense lines of her face easing. Even her pursed lips tipped up into a thoughtful smile.

"Parker hit on me in a bar and he was one of the most beautiful men I'd ever seen before. And believe me, I've seen some pretty boys. But he had this rugged manliness that just appealed to me. He had more scars on his hands than I'd ever seen on any man and that ... usefulness was something I'd never seen before."

She laughed and glanced at him again. "You ever just get this feeling like things are happening for a reason? And even though the entire world shouts that you're wrong for each other, you just have to be together?"

Mac looked out the window, losing his breath. Many years ago maybe, but not for a long time. "How long were you together?"

She shook her head and ran a hand through her ultra-feminine hair. "Almost two weeks. Then we let some crazy argument get out of hand and we parted ways. I think we both knew that our relationship wasn't going anywhere. I mean, he was in the SEALs in Virginia and I was going to school in Boston."

"Which aren't especially far apart," he commented.

"I know," she whispered. "But I think we were both scared that it was so perfect. It was one of those 'rip the Band Aid off quick and get it over with' things."

Mac left her in her own mind for a few minutes. "And how did you come together again?"

Andromeda swallowed. "As I was getting off the elevator in the parking garage this morning a woman attacked me. I fought her off but there was a man, too. I got in my car and drove through a gate to break out of my building's parking garage." She glanced at him from the corners of her eyes. "They're probably going to up my rates."

Mac could see past the humor to the lingering fear in her. Andromeda was not the type of woman to engage in fighting of any kind. But she'd impressed him today with her spunk. And she needed to know that, he decided. "Well, it doesn't sound like you had any choice in the matter. You did exactly what needed done, so don't agonize over it."

She gave him a grateful smile. "Thank you, Mac. I know this thing has turned your world upside down, but I appreciate everything you're doing to secure my case."

He nodded his head and they settled into silence.

———

Parker knew he was dreaming, but he didn't know how to get out of it. Seeing Andy had stirred things inside him that he'd thought he'd gotten over.

Parker knew what she wanted. He could see it in her eyes. She wanted him to stay with her, but there was no way he could. Yeah, he might have a couple more days to fuck around but his leave would be over soon, and he'd be heading right back into the jungle.

If there was a woman worth giving up his career for, though, Andromeda Pierce was right there at the top of his short list. The woman was incredible. Self-assured and competent, she didn't come with ninety-eight percent of the baggage that other women did. And that was more refreshing than he could have ever expected.

The sex was fucking amazing, though. The guys rode him hard about disappearing every night, but he had to have as much of her as he could. There was a huge countdown clock in his head, ticking down to zero faster and faster.

Parker rocked his head and saw Andy sitting at a chair in the kitchen in her apartment. There were tears streaking down her cheeks, and she seemed pissed that she'd let them be seen. He leaned back into the room to yell something and she tipped her chin up, arms crossed beneath her lovely breasts, long hair behind her shoulders.

Parker had never yelled at a woman before. Ever. And he felt like shit for doing it now. He was just soooo frustrated.

Andy wiped the tears from her cheeks, but she didn't say anything as he turned to leave. Parker hesitated at the door, praying she would say something. But she didn't. So, he walked out the door and out of her life.

He'd been hell on wheels for months afterward, but he'd been too stubborn to do anything about it. For months his guys cajoled, distracted, basically did everything they could to get his mind off of her. The only relief he had was when they were in country. Then he was completely focused on the mission ahead of him.

Rolling his head, he looked at the guy beside him. Chico had one of the better dispositions, but something that day irritated him. As soon as Parker had settled into the dirt beside him Chico's mood had gone downhill.

"What crawled up your ass and died?" he asked, aggravated.

"You did, man. You bring bad juju with you. I don' wanna be near it."

Being a Navy Seal was a brotherhood like no other. To have a fellow SEAL say he didn't want to be around him hurt, almost as bad as breaking up with Andy.

He supposed if he was telling the truth he wouldn't want to be with him either.

Then that fucker Sarfraz was there, grinning his rotten-toothed smile as he walked toward Parker with a fucking sledgehammer in his hand this time. His heart began to race, and he struggled against the cable ties holding his wrists to the floor. He knew he couldn't break them, but he also couldn't just accept what the interrogator was about to do. He had to fight. The man laughed at his struggles, smoothly brought the sledge up over his head, then brought it down with all his strength. Parker screamed.

He smelled gun oil.

Glancing around, he looked for the source of the smell. Oh, his M4 was on his bed in about five hundred pieces. It actually wasn't that many, but when you were bone-tired and needed to lay down, but you had to put the rifle back together before you could do anything, it was a load of shit.

With a few quick twists of his hands, the M4 was together again and he was sighting down its length. Then he was falling into his rack.

But he didn't, actually. He landed on his stomach on the desert floor, biting ants crawling all around him. Parker tried to brush them away, but they kept finding new ways to bite him.

"Well," Andy tilted her head. "If you'd stayed with me it wouldn't have happened."

Parker blinked his eyes open, wondering what was real and what wasn't. Gravity shifted and he felt like he was in a decelerating boat. He scanned the roof. Oh, maybe just a car. There were trees out the window, but that's all he could see.

Looking down, he realized his hand was resting on where he was aching. There was a mound of something over the pain. Craning his neck, he looked down the length of his body. He was laying diagonally in the back of a vehicle and his gut had been patched with something. What the hell was that?

They were decelerating again. He reached out for something to hold onto, but he couldn't find anything to grip. He ended up bracing himself on the driver's seat with his arms over his head.

A man with reddish beard hair looked back at him, and details started to filter in. This was Mac and they were supposed to be protecting Mac for a court case. Parker looked up into the driver's seat and his heart stopped.

There she was. Even upside down she was the most beautiful thing he'd ever seen. He loved her haircut. It was edgy and spunky and made her appear soft, though she'd probably meant for it to do the exact opposite.

The vehicle they were riding in turned and he had to brace again. Mac reached back a hand and pressed down on his shoulder, which helped a bit. Kept him from rocking and hurting. And he needed it because this road was going to kill him. Against his will he gasped aloud in pain.

"I'm so sorry, Parker. I'll slow down."

She did, and the jostling wasn't so bad. He lost time as they continued, and he eventually realized they were going uphill. Then it got even steeper and the tires began to spin, even though he could tell she'd switched into four-wheel drive. One rise they went up was steep enough that he could see out of the rear window, but all he saw were trees. Miles upon miles of trees. Then the road leveled out and she picked up some speed.

"That's strange," she murmured. "I thought Rosalind was in Georgia."

Adrenaline spiked through him and he levered himself

up in spite of the pain in his side. They were on a mountain-top, with only trees and mountains as far as the eyes could see. Directly ahead of them was a long, low cabin, rustic and homey. Another SUV sat parked out front.

"Are you sure it's her car?" he demanded.

"Yes, I'm sure."

They parked the vehicle behind the other one. Andromeda circled to the back to open the hatch and Parker pushed himself out. His head was woozy but he forced himself to stand. He looked up into the business end of a shotgun.

CHAPTER 7

"I'm NOT sure why you have a hold on my girl like that, but you need to let her go."

Andromeda looked down. She hadn't even noticed Parker's grip on her upper arm. "Oh, he's okay, Roz. This is Parker Quinn. Remember, *Parker?*"

The woman on the porch lowered the shotgun, but she was still frowning. "Okay..."

Andromeda pulled away from Parker to climb the steps to hug her friend. Roz lowered the shotgun to her side and gave her a one-armed hug, but still kept her gaze on the two men. "What's going on, Andromeda?"

She blinked down into her friend's kind eyes and struggled with her emotions. It would be so easy to cry on Roz's shoulder, but they had stuff to do. "Do you have any medical equipment here with you?"

Roz blinked, her dark brows lowering over cornflower blue eyes. "You know I do. Why?"

"Because Parker's been shot."

All eyes focused on Parker and he gave a snort, even as he reached out to lean upon the car.

Sighing, Roz leaned her shotgun against the porch railing and went down the steps. "And who are you?"

Mac seemed startled when she looked at him. "Mac."

"He's my witness and I'm trying to keep him safe," Andromeda explained. "Parker was at my condo protecting me and he got shot when we went to find Mac."

Roz spared her a glance. "Sounds like a very truncated version of what's happened."

Andromeda barked out a laugh as she took one of Parker's arms around her shoulders. "Very."

Roz stepped under Parker's other arm and they walked him to the steps. He seemed to stagger at one point, almost pulling them down and Mac took over from Roz. He carried him up the steps and into the darkness of the cabin like it wasn't anything.

"I want him on the table."

Roz rushed across to the wide-planked table, snatching a blanket from the couch as she passed to cover the surface. Parker groaned as he lay down on the table and she wanted to cry out with him, but it wouldn't do anyone any good. Andromeda stood back as Roz went to work.

Before they'd met, Roz had been a nurse at Riverglade Hospital in Columbus, in the emergency department. Andromeda remembered the details like the case was yesterday. They'd had a crazy drunk come in and he'd been placed under a psychiatric hold, but they'd had problems finding him a bed. It had been flu season that year and the hospital was woefully overcrowded. So, they'd kept him in the emergency department longer than they should have. Roz had gone in to check on him at one point and he'd hit her as soon as she'd walked into the room, knocking her out cold. She didn't come to until he'd penetrated her on the bathroom floor. She'd fought and bit, but she hadn't been able to fight him off. But she had been able to reach the nurse call cord hanging near the toilet. Within minutes she had people there. The orderlies fought with the homeless man, but the damage had already been already done. Roz had cooperated fully in the prosecution, but she hadn't been able to go back to the hospital where she'd been attacked. Andromeda didn't think she'd have had been able to go back either.

But she could see how good of a nurse Roz had been. Parker had passed out again, which made everything easier as she unwrapped the 'bandage'. "Pads? Really?"

"It's a military thing," Mac rumbled.

She stared at him for a moment before turning back to Parker. She pulled a stethoscope from her bag and took a quick blood pressure. "It looks clean through. Most of the bleeding has stopped but he's low on volume."

She rummaged in her pack, pulling out an IV setup. She handed the fluid bag to Mac. "Hold this up until I can think of a way to rig it."

He took it from her without a word and did as he was told. Then she hooked the IV into Parker's hand. "He'll probably need a couple bags. Antibiotics. Pain management. I assume there's a reason why you can't go to a hospital."

"If they're tracking us we can't go to a hospital. That would be on the news."

"Hm. Probably right."

She worked for several long minutes and Andromeda just stood back and watched. Roz looked up at her at one point with a questioning look. Andromeda leaned forward to look down at his body.

Roz had stripped most of his clothing off and his body was gorgeous and muscular, until you realized it was *covered* in scars. Not just a few here and there but hundreds of measured cuts covered his body, ranging in lengths from a few centimeters to several inches. Andromeda nodded to her, indicating that she'd seen these, then her gaze drifted lower. Roz had left his athletic boxers on, but there were faint silver lines going beneath the fabric. Then she got to his legs. Here there were larger surgical scars where they had apparently gone in to fix his legs.

"My God," Roz breathed. "Who could have done all this to him?"

"I don't know."

Roz flung a sheet out over top of him, then gave her a direct look. "He'll be fine, Andromeda. He'll be hurting for the next few days, but he'll be all right."

Andromeda moved close enough to grasp his free hand. He hadn't roused since they'd entered the house. She wanted, needed, to see his eyes. It had been a crazy day with even more crazy ups and downs. Parker reappearing in her life was definitely an 'up', but he would leave her with a devastating 'down'. Been there and done that, but it didn't keep her from reaching out to run her fingers through his short dirty blond hair and down his bruised cheek.

What the hell was she supposed to do with him?

As she looked at his big body stretched out on the table, she was very thankful that Roz had been here.

"I thought you were in Georgia."

Roz looked up at her as she readied suture material. "I was, but things fell in line and something told me I needed to leave early. I understand why now. It's good to see you in one piece, Andromeda."

"It's good to be in one piece."

"Why don't you tell me what happened while I stitch this guy up?"

It was a reasonable request, so Andromeda told her about their day. Several times Roz stopped to stare at her in disbelief.

Andromeda stopped talking just as Roz tied the last stitch. She gathered up stray bits of trash, then dropped her gloves into the trash can. She took the IV bag from Mac and hung it up over the swaying light fixture.

"I need wine," she said finally, turning away.

Andromeda knew where the glasses were. Retrieving three from the cupboard she set them on the counter. "Do you mind if I hop in the shower real quick? I was rolling on the garage floor and I've got Parker's blood all over me."

"Of course," Roz agreed softly. "If you need something to wear you know where everything is."

Andromeda flipped her hand in a quick wave as she walked away. Since they hadn't stopped anywhere after the truck stop, she would definitely need to borrow something until she could wash up what she was wearing. The black slacks would be fine after a good wash, but the maroon sweater was wrecked. She let both puddle in the corner of the bathroom as she started the water to let it warm.

As she stepped beneath the shower head, every tight, strained muscle began to relax. A streak of fire went down her arm and she craned her head to look around. Oh, damn, she'd been cut. Probably not enough to get stitched but definitely enough it should probably be cleaned out.

Ducking her head beneath the water, she thought about everything that had happened. It would be smart to sit down and write everything out while it was fresh in her mind. As soon as she had a moment to herself she would dig her laptop out and typed a few things up.

Right now, the water felt too good to leave.

CHAPTER 8

Roz LOOKED at her trashed house. How had to gone from nice and neat and calm to dangerous and trashed in less than an hour?

She looked at the big man standing in her kitchen and a shiver of anxiety went through her. "Uh, there's a wine fridge there by your legs. Why don't you pick out a bottle while I stoke the fire?"

He moved to do as she asked and as she broke up kindling she could hear him rummaging in the drawers looking for an opener. "It's hanging on the wall by the sink," she called.

"Found it. Thank you."

Roz got a steady flame going, then stood by the mantle wondering what she should do. There was no way she was walking back in there to talk to the man. What had Andromeda been thinking leaving him here for her to entertain?

No, Andromeda wouldn't have brought someone into her home that wasn't okay. If she left him here he had to be a trustworthy guy, right? She could go in and get the wine then come right back out here. There was an exit on each end of the room, as well as plenty of things she could use as a weapon.

"You can do this," she whispered to herself.

Marching into the kitchen she grabbed the wine glass from the counter and then the bottle he'd chosen. The man had moved to the window to look outside, giving her several feet of space. Pouring the deep red into the glass she moved to leave, but he turned to her.

"I'm sorry we've put you out."

Roz shook her head. "I'm not put out. A little freaked by all the people invading my space, but I can deal with it."

The big man ran his hand over his reddish beard. "I understand completely, and I will try to keep my footprint small."

Roz frowned, realizing how cold her voice had sounded to him. "I don't mean to sound bitchy. I just... don't prefer to be around m...people."

His expression eased into a polite smile, like he hadn't even noticed her slip. "I know exactly what you mean. I don't either. I might scout around outside if you don't mind."

She waved her free hand. "Have fun. The entire mountain is mine to the power line clearing."

He doffed his hat to her and moved for the door. She had an attack of conscience and cringed. "Don't be gone too long. Andromeda will freak."

"Agreed," he said softly, and moved out the door.

Roz watched the big man go. He hadn't made a sound, even though it looked like he had ten pounds of junk in that pocketed vest thing. He needed a pipe in his mouth or something to chew on. Hopefully he had a compass because she really didn't want to go find his ass late at night.

The pipes rattled as Andromeda turned her shower off.

Crossing the room to her dining room table she checked on her patient, but he was sleeping deeply, as she'd expected. The light sedative she'd given him would help him sleep easier. The wound wasn't life threatening now, though he had lost a lot of blood. And he had a bit of a fever, but the antibiotics would beat that off.

She could see why Andy had been so gone on him. The guy was a hunk. There were scars on his body, though, that you didn't get from sitting at a desk. This man got out and did the hard work that the country needed. She'd counted three other gunshot wounds on him, as well as several other apparent knife wounds. She'd seen her fair share of both when she'd been in Columbus. For a moment when she'd been treating him it had been like she'd never left. She kept her certifications up, but that was it. She lived comfortably off the settlement money the hospital had been ordered to pay, so she certainly didn't need a job.

As she glanced down the man's body, she had to admit it had gotten her blood pumping a bit.

Roz took a sip of her wine as she walked into the living room and settled onto the couch. In a way this was going to work out for her. For some reason she'd been craving human interaction recently. Her twenty-year old son was going to college in Atlanta and she'd always stuck close for him, in case he needed her. But recently, he'd been relying more on his friends and acquaintances than her.

Was this just an empty-nest issue? She looked through the window and out at the vista before her. That view was precious to her. And she couldn't imagine giving it up just because she missed talking with someone about the weather. That view had saved her sanity over the years.

Now, there were two men on her mountain, when there never had been before. That put her on edge.

Andy came through the hallway, her eyes going immediately to the man still laying on the table. She glanced at Roz. "Is he doing okay?"

Roz nodded. "He'll be fine with some rest and medications. You don't need to worry about him."

Andromeda crossed the room and went down on her knees in front of the couch, then she wrapped Roz in a huge, bony hug. Roz returned the hug gratefully, her eyes filling with tears. "You need to gain some weight, woman," she groused, prodding at Andromeda's bicep as she pulled away.

Andy laughed and gripped her hands in her own. "Whatever. You always tell me that."

"It's always true. What's the last thing you ate today?"

Andy screwed up her face in thought. "Gummy bears?"

Roz could have gagged. "That is so wrong. You need actual food."

Andy shrugged her shoulders. "Had other things on my mind," she admitted. "Oh, can you bandage this for me? It's in such an awkward spot."

She turned her arm and showed her a long gash. Roz felt terrible for not even noticing it. "Oh, damn. Yes, let's get this cleaned up."

Pushing off the couch she headed over to the med kit on the floor. She disinfected the cut and looked at it in the light of the window. It wasn't deep enough to require stitches, but it would definitely be irritating to heal up. "I'm going to superglue this one."

She applied the fast setting glue and held it until it sealed. "That will keep out debris and stuff. If you feel it split, let me know and we'll do it again."

Andromeda didn't know what she'd do without Roz in her life. She turned and gave the woman another hug, seriously happy to see her in the flesh. Texts and emails were fine but seeing a person *in person* was so much better. "How have you been? How's Tyler?"

Roz rolled her eyes. "He's too good to answer his mom's texts and calls. That was part of why I came up here. I was tired of being ignored and discounted."

Andromeda laughed. "Well, he's a big college student now. He doesn't have time to be coddled by his mother."

"I don't coddle him, but I do keep tabs on him. Or I try to."

Tyler had been one of those kids that had barely scraped through high school, but he was suddenly loving college. He had no goal in mind other than to try everything. Andromeda would have been frustrated too. "Well, I can't tell you how happy I am you were here. Eventually I probably would have had to take Parker in to the hospital and we all would have been in danger. Thank you for patching him up here."

Her friend smiled, the creases around her eyes deepening. "No problem. Although I will admit to being a little on edge that you brought two strange men to my mountain."

Andromeda cringed. "I know. I'm very sorry. This would never have been an option if I thought the men were even the slightest bit dangerous." She paused. "Let me say that differently. If I thought they were the slightest danger to *you*, this would not have even been an option."

And it wouldn't have been. They'd have found somewhere else to chill and allow Parker to recuperate.

"Parker is a good guy. A little too devoted to a different lifestyle for my taste, but his heart was always solid gold. And Mac, well, he's former military as well but he has the most calming personality. I can't imagine him ever fighting in a war, now. He'd rather just get lost in his books and research. He has a liberal studies doctorate as well as a biology degree. This situation isn't anything he chose for himself, but he had vital information and he stepped up to volunteer it. Even as we were running for our lives he kept his cool. He's a practical, useful bookworm. He might want to raid your book shelves."

Roz sighed. "I might let him, I guess. Wine?"

"Hell, yes!"

CHAPTER 9

PARKER OPENED his eyes a few hours later. Again, he was disoriented looking up at a swaying light fixture. Looked like something you'd see over a kitchen table. But it had an IV fluid bag hanging from it.

Rocking his head, he looked around. Was this the cabin where they'd pulled up earlier? It about had to be. Blinking the sleep from his eyes he lifted a hand to rub at his dry eyes, then blinked them open again.

He seemed to be in a kitchen, laying on a hard as fuck table. His legs were throbbing with pain. He lifted up on one elbow and waited for his head to stop spinning and his gut to stop twinging. It was quivering like a muscle that had been over exercised, but the pain was manageable. Using his arms, he pushed to a sitting position.

Yeah, he could do this.

Parker heard voices murmuring to his right. One sounded like Andromeda, and there was a deeper woman's voice he didn't recognize. Was that the shotgun lady?

Sliding off the edge of the table he put first one foot down, then the other. As his weight settled onto his better left leg, he winced in pain. It had been too long since he'd been vertical. Even as he thought it, he started to get a cramp in his right calf.

"Fuck."

He knew if he bent down there was a chance he'd go ass over tea kettle. The cramp would go away in a minute. It would.

Andromeda gasped when she came in and he opened his eyes. What a lame fuck she must think he was. They had basically taken care of him for the entire day. He glanced out the window. The sun was going down soon, and it had been morning when they'd picked up Mac.

"Is your witness okay?" he demanded.

She nodded, walking toward him. "Yes, he's fine. He's outside communing with nature, like he does every day. Are you okay?"

Parker forced a nod, even as he tried to stretch out his toes. The cramp tightened more painfully, and he grimaced.

"What is it, Parker? Tell me!"

"Cramp," he gasped.

She looked down and before he could say anything she'd started massaging the quivering muscle. He'd have cried out in pain, but he still had some pride and he bit it off. Her long fingers moved up and down his calf and he had to admit it felt better than just suffering through it.

It felt good enough that he began to notice the position she was in.

Could he be any more humiliated?

Grabbing the blanket he'd been laying upon, he wrapped it around his hips. "I think I'm okay, Andy. Thank you."

She looked up at him, her golden eyes full of worry. Giving her a hand, he pulled her to her feet, but she didn't step away. Instead she took a step forward, planting her feet outside of his own, and wrapped her arms around him.

Parker had dreamt about having Andromeda in his arms almost constantly since he'd gotten the call a few days ago. But his dreams didn't compare to how she actually felt. She buried her face into his neck and he wrapped his arms around her shoulders, burying his nose into her hair. Thoughts of when they'd been together crowded into his brain. There had been so many good times.

Her hands stroked his back. "I was worried about you."

"Meh, I knew I was good. As long as the bullet goes through you're okay."

She pulled back to give him a frowning look. "So, the other three bullets you've taken have all gone through?"

He laughed, then clutched his side. "Okay, you caught me. No, none of the others did. That was why they knocked me out of the game for so long."

She shook her head at him, then her fingers were running over his jaw. Angling the tips of her fingers she let the nails scrape against his whiskers, something they'd both loved years ago.

Parker didn't know what to do. She felt so good in his arms, but there was no sense in encouraging anything. He had a life in Colorado, now, and she was very firmly ensconced in Columbus. She had a solid career path and he would never interfere with that.

She seemed to realize how dangerous she was being, because she stepped back. Parker let the rest of his weight settle onto his right leg, needing the pain to bring him back to reality. It did exactly that. Clenching his teeth, he snugged the blanket around his hips. "Thank you for saving me from your friend."

Andy grinned, her broad smile almost blinding to him.

"You're welcome. It was a near thing. Luckily she's more inclined to save lives than take them."

"For now," an alto voice agreed. "Cross me and I'll give you another scar, and I'll make sure it doesn't go through."

Parker grinned, liking the matter-of-fact woman a lot. She was short and petite, but strong willed. She reached out and took his hand in her own.

"Why don't you sit down before you fall down? Rosalind White."

"Parker Quinn," he told her, settling into the chair she pulled out for him.

"Andromeda, why don't you get Mr. Quinn a bottle of water?"

Andy moved to do as the older woman suggested. Parker was impressed. He took the water bottle she handed him, only realizing then how thirsty he was. With a few heavy swallows he drank the bottle down.

"I wouldn't drink any more than that," Roz cautioned.

Yeah, he thought that too.

"Where are we?" he asked, looking out the window, then back to Andy.

"West Virginia."

His brows shot up in surprise, but she didn't flinch.

"That's a long way from Columbus."

Andy shrugged.

"Not really. A few hours. It's no big deal."

"Are you confident we weren't followed?"

She shrugged her narrow shoulders. "As confident as Mac and I can be."

Well, that was as much as they could hope for, he supposed.

"I told Mike I would email him when we got settled."

Parker nodded. That made sense.

Rosalind moved to the fridge and peered into the freezer. She rummaged around for a moment before pulling out a blue bag. "I'll have some dinner made within the next hour."

"I can help."

Parker watched the two women together. It was obvious they were very good friends because they talked about subject after subject without pause, all the while getting a delicious smelling dinner together. Parker's stomach growled. It had been a day since he'd eaten anything, and he was really feeling the lack.

The medical equipment was cleared away and Roz took him off the IV. "As long as you keep drinking and taking in nutrients I think you'll be fine."

Andy set a tall glass of water in front of him and he gave her a smile. She turned away quickly.

A half hour later when she set the plate of food in front of him, he grabbed her hand before she could pull away. Her eyes flicked to his. "Are you doing okay?"

She nodded and pulled her fingers from his. "I'm going to go see where Mac is."

Parker didn't say anything, just watched her go through the front door and out onto the porch. As soon as she closed the door behind herself he was pushing up out of the chair.

"Hey, now," Roz started, but he waved her away.

"I'm good. Going to go take a piss."

She gave him a narrow-eyed look then nodded her chin out the window. "There's a reading area about a hundred and fifty yards to the west. That's probably where they'll be." She pointed a finger at him. "Don't make me have to carry your ass. Stay on the trail."

Parker gave her a grin and a wink, then followed Andy.

Walking wasn't too bad. There had been pain when

he'd pushed up from the table but it was manageable. He probably still had some pain killer running through his veins. When it ran out in a few hours, he might be singing a different song though.

There was a well-worn path to the right, through the side yard and into the woods. Before he followed the obvious trail he did a little reconnoitering. The cabin sat in the middle of a clearing. Trees of all kinds surrounded the property, all losing their leaves. The fading colors were beautiful, though. Vibrant and startling against the fading light in the sky.

There was a small outbuilding with a portable generator inside, as well as a huge tank to fuel it. Parker glanced at the fuel gage. Roz was a smart woman. She could be trapped up here for weeks and with this much fuel it didn't matter. She'd be fine.

Circling the house, he looked for weaknesses, but there weren't many. Roz had a sturdy little escape here. Andy had said she'd been a client before they'd been friends and he had to wonder what kind of client.

Parker paused at the vehicles to look down the rutted track of a driveway. Your average passenger car would not make it up that. Hell, he bet even the four-wheel drives struggled. Leaning back against the car for a moment, he drew in a few deep breaths. It felt good to be outside. Reaching into Andromeda's car he found the bag he'd grabbed early this morning from his truck. There was a lot of blood inside the car. When he felt better he needed to get out here and clean it up.

Setting the bag on the hood of her car he pulled out a spare pair of jeans and a t-shirt. Bending over was out so he had to finagle the jeans carefully before pulling them up his hips. The shirt was easier, but he was still out of breath by the time he was done. Removing his spare weapon, he slipped it into the back waistband of his pants. He'd have to ask Andy what she'd done with his other gun.

He started down the path Roz had directed him to. He was a hundred feet in when he met Mac on the path. The other man seemed surprised to see him on his feet. Parker gave him a smile. "I'm hard to keep down."

Mac grinned at him and held out his hand. "It's good, though. I was worried you were done for."

"Nah. You know as well as I do when you have a mission, you take a licking and keep on ticking."

Mac gave him an ironic nod. "Isn't that the truth?"

"Roz has some dinner ready if you're interested."

Mac smiled slightly. "That's what Andromeda said." He made a motion down the path. "She asked for some privacy."

Parker looked down the path, wondering if that request applied to him. "You don't know where my gun went, do you?"

Without a word, Mac reached behind his back and pulled out Parker's HK, handing it over. Parker looked at it in surprise, then up at Mac. The older man shrugged uncomfortably. "Seemed prudent to stay armed. I cleaned it for you, but you only have one mag. Must have reloaded in the park and dropped your empty."

Parker nodded. "I did," he said slowly. "I have more mags in my bag. Thank you."

Without a word, Mac tipped his hat and turned toward the cabin.

"Hey, Mac."

The other man turned to look at him and Parker held out his backup weapon. "If you're comfortable..."

Mac looked at the gun for a long time and Parker wondered how long ago he'd gotten out of the service.

Maybe it wasn't old hat anymore and he didn't want the responsibility.

Mac took the weapon with a heavy sigh and checked it, then slipped it into a hidden spot. Touching his fingers to the brim of his hat, he turned for the cabin.

Parker stared after him thoughtfully. Andy had said that he was a former Green Beret. Guess that old training had kicked in.

The path away from the cabin was easy to follow. It was obvious it had been used well over the years. He misstepped on a stone and cranked his left ankle, his weak one. That pain radiated up into his gut and he had to pause for a moment to catch his breath. He used to run on shit worse than this barefoot, but at thirty-five, and today especially, he felt like an old man.

He looked around, but the trees seemed to stretch a long ways. The trail curved down and to the right and there was a huge truck-sized boulder at the side of the trail he couldn't see around. His energy was beginning to wane and he felt like a pussy, tiring out so easily.

Then he heard her. All of his own worries disappeared as he caught the sound of her sobbing. Rounding the boulder, his gaze roved the small stream he'd found. There, over a small bridge was a beautiful little gazebo. He had to stare for a moment because he couldn't believe it was here. But it wasn't just a gazebo. There were panels on the sides that appeared to be for blocking out the weather. They were all up and open right now, like weird petals of a flower.

Parker was used to seeing benches inside a gazebo but this one was different. There were benches on one side, but on the other were two divan, couch things. Like fainting couches. There was a desk along the backside and solar powered fairy lights hung from the rafters. This was probably a pretty cool place at night. There was an empty fire ring at the edge of the stream, directly in sight of the couches.

Andy sat curled up on one of the long benches, arms around her drawn-up knees as she wept. She didn't startle when he reached out to stroke her back, just turned into his arms. Parker hesitated for only a moment, wishing he could be a better man for her.

ANDROMEDA KNEW HE WOULD COME. He should have been flat on his back after being shot, but Parker Quinn didn't roll like that. He never had. He would overcome any obstacle put in front of him, sometimes at the expense of himself and others. It was one of the things she admired most about him. It was also what she hated the most.

But as his strong arms wrapped around her back and his fingers grazed her cheeks, she forgot about all their old baggage. Parker had one of the most incredible hugs, warm and solid. Exactly what a woman emotionally well beyond her breaking point needed.

He didn't ask her what was wrong or how he could fix it, he just held her. The position had to be a little awkward for him, but he didn't say a word.

Andromeda knew she needed to get a hold of herself, but she'd just been so wrung out. It had been a traumatic day for her. Between the attack first thing this morning, and the shooting and the drive to West Virginia, she was at her wits' end. And this was the perfect place to let down her guard, where no one could see the professional, controlled Andromeda Pierce lose her shit.

Eventually, she reached the end of her tears and she

pulled back to look up into Parker's face. He grinned down at her a little sleepily. "Better?"

She nodded, wiping beneath her eyes for the last time. "I'm good. I'm sorry."

"Don't be sorry. You didn't do anything wrong."

She pulled away and straightened on the side of the bench. Parker straightened as well, stroking a hand down her back. "We all have a breaking point, Andy. You had a monster day today. No one will say a word. Including me. It's all good."

She cleared her throat. "Thank you, Parker."

"If they ask questions," he said, taking her hand in his own, "you can tell them we were having sex."

Andromeda burst into startled laughter even as a flush of warmth rolled through her. "What?"

"You heard me."

She blinked into his grinning face and for a fleeting moment, thought about taking him up on his suggestion. Then she snatched her hand away. "You are so bad! Just like you used to be."

"Well, we had a lot of good sex back then. It ruled my life for a while."

Yeah, it had ruled hers too.

"Still, we can't do that. You were shot just hours ago."

Parker gave her a look. "Believe me, if you told me I could have you on this bench right this second, I would be man enough for the job."

Laughing, Andromeda shook her head, feeling tickled and a little flushed. "You are incorrigible."

That had been one of the things that had drawn her to Parker years ago, that playful irreverence. It was exactly opposite of her practical nature. But she was smart enough to know that that playfulness had been what had drawn her to him. Her life was planned down to the minute and the goal and the milestone. He made her forget all that. For two weeks they'd spent every spare minute together. It was the best time she'd ever had.

That had been a long time ago, though. Years. And her life hadn't changed so much. She was still goal driven and determined to live a certain way.

The lines on Parker's face and the way he moved told her that Parker had seen hard times, so she was glad he could still play around.

"Maybe we should head back to the cabin."

He sighed, looking out at the stream. "Mind if we sit here a bit? It's peaceful."

Oh, yeah. He *had* just been shot.

"That's fine."

They sat for several long minutes not saying anything and it was actually nice.

"How long have you known Roz? She seems like a fire-cracker."

Andromeda laughed. "Oh, she is, believe me. But she's my best friend."

"When did you meet her? I don't remember you talking about a Roz."

"Mm. I just met her a few years ago. I prosecuted her case. She'd been horribly attacked while on duty at a hospital. She filed against the hospital because they were criminally liable for not having a place to house patients deemed mentally unstable in the ER. They actually had plans for a space, had promised it to the ER several times, but they'd pushed it off for a couple of years because the administrators thought they needed pay raises more. She walked into my office with all of the paperwork in hand and they came back with a settlement a week after I filed charges against them. They knew they were in the wrong and had been caught with their pants down."

"Damn. She sounds like a powerhouse."

Andromeda grinned. "She is. We clicked immediately because even though she portrays herself one way, she has the heart of a gummy bear. It took her a long time to recover after the attack. She stayed with me for a while because of the security at my condo. We drank a lot of wine together and commiserated on things we could and couldn't change. Part of her settlement was that the hospital had to get that protective space done within three months. And they did. It was down to the minute, but they got it done."

"But she doesn't work there now?"

Andromeda shook her head, her heart aching for her friend. "She couldn't go back to work there. She tried, but there were too many bad memories. The guy, well, he hurt her bad and even as strong as she is, her PTSD made it so she just couldn't handle it. After the settlement she resigned to take care of her son, but last year he headed off to college. I think she's been picking up a few hours here and there at some of the local clinics to keep her certifications up to date, but she doesn't need the job."

"Sounds like she needs a purpose."

"Yes," she sighed. "I try to come down as much as I can. But I have a lot on my plate right now. I'm in line for a promotion. If I can tie this al Fareq case up, it would go a long way to cementing my career path."

She turned to him on the bench, the light fading through the trees around them. "And what about you? I never heard anything out of you after you left." She tried to keep her words light, but they may have come out sounding a little accusatory.

"I went back to my SEAL team. We shot up a lot of shit and saved a bunch of people."

She frowned when he stopped because she knew there was more, but he was being difficult about this. In essence he was reminding her exactly what she *hadn't* missed about him. "Well, okay then. Guess we should be getting back to the cabin."

Andromeda moved to push up off the bench, but Parker stopped her with a hand on her arm. "I'm sorry, Andy. I'm not..."

She waved a hand. "No worries. I'm good. I appreciate the reminder."

He frowned. "What reminder?"

"That you won't be around very long."

Andromeda stepped down out of the gazebo, her gaze running up the bubbling stream. Her heart had been wrong when she'd heard that he was no longer a SEAL. For one tiny moment in time she'd thought maybe there was a chance for something between them.

Which was crazy. He'd been back in her life exactly twelve hours.

Parker Quinn would just have to continue being the one that got away.

CHAPTER 10

MAC WALKED into the house wondering what kind of reception he'd get. Roz seemed temperamental and wary of men, and he didn't want to spook her in any way. He made sure to shut the door loudly enough that she would surely hear.

Roz peered around the doorway at him. "Hey. There's food if you're hungry."

Then she ducked away. Mac took his shoes off and set them by the door, then hung his hat on one of the coat hooks. He smoothed his hair but he knew it had to be wild. It had been a while since he'd bothered to get a haircut. He'd planned to do it before he went to testify in court.

Mac walked into the kitchen and she shoved a plate at him as she walked past. "Help yourself to anything on the stove. Parker has already eaten. I'm going to make the bedrooms up."

Mac watched her go, wondering what he'd done to piss her off. And if it was worth trying to change her mind.

He helped himself to the chicken and vegetables she'd made. There were rolls on the table and he buttered one up, then groaned in pleasure as he began to chew. He'd never had better tasting bread. Setting the plate on the table, he wondered if it would be rude to eat just the bread for dinner. There was a jar of blackberry preserves on the table as well. That would be dessert.

When he was done eating he pushed away from the table and crossed to the sink. Roz hadn't done the dishes yet and there was no washer, per se, so he would wash them. Maybe if he did that she would give him the recipe for the rolls and the jelly.

Mac glanced up when she reentered the room and he offered her a smile. "The food was very good. Thank you. But the rolls were sublime. Did you make those?"

He turned back to the sink, fearing that if he kept looking at her she wouldn't answer.

"I did. It's an old family recipe."

"Is it shareable? Or one of those things that you'll only pass on to a blood relative? Because I would be willing to swap some blood with you for it."

She glanced at him sharply and he made sure to keep his expression eager and a little playful.

"Do you cook?"

"I try," he admitted. "Bread is one of the few things I've managed to become adept at." He reached into his left-hand pocket to show her the paperback he was carrying right then. "Gives me time to read in between the steps."

Roz barked out a laugh and crossed her arms. "What's your best recipe?"

Mac knew a challenge when he heard one, and he was ready for it. "Well, my Parker House rolls make your taste buds sing, but I prefer making baguettes. They're good with everything and they took me a long time to perfect."

She frowned at him in consideration. "I'll think about it,"

she said eventually. "And thank you, I'm glad you enjoyed them. They are my son's favorite."

"Mm. I can understand why. They melted in my mouth. And the jelly." He shook his head. "Ambrosia."

Her eyes widened at that and her expression softened a little. "Thank you. It's been a while since anyone has appreciated my cooking. Those berries grow wild on the mountain."

Knowing when he'd won a round, Mac turned back to the sink to finish the dishes. He was extremely surprised when she took up a dishtowel and started drying, but he tried not to let her see. Instead, he kept washing like he'd been doing and handing the dishes off to her. Within just a few minutes they were done. Mac wished he had more to wash.

"I'll leave the food out for a few more minutes in case they come back," she murmured, "then I'll put it away."

Mac crossed to the table and drank the last of his wine, then returned to the sink to rinse the glass. "I love your reading spot," he told her softly.

She didn't say anything for a long time, so he wiped down the sink and the counter on his side, looking out at the darkening night or the kitchen, anywhere but at her. If he looked at her he knew instinctively that she would spook.

"Thank you," she said finally. "It is my refuge."

"I can understand why."

Roz left the kitchen but returned a few minutes later. "I can show you where you'll sleep."

The tiredness he'd been staving off hit him then and he followed her without a word. It looked like there were a few bedrooms back here.

"The bathroom is here, and this room will be yours. Sorry you have to share."

She motioned to the door but didn't step close enough to him to open it. Mac opened the door himself and stepped through. It wasn't a big room but each of the twin beds had homemade quilts across them. It looked comfortable enough. "Thank you."

"I, uh, know you don't have clothes to change into and I'm sorry I don't have anything, but I did have spare toothbrushes. There are three new ones on the sink."

Mac was touched. That was more consideration than he'd gotten for a long time.

"Thank you, Roz. I really appreciate you opening up your home to us."

Without a word she headed down the hallway to the bedroom door on the end. He assumed that was her room. When she let herself inside her gaze connected to his for a split second before she closed the door and he heard a deadbolt slide home.

A deadbolt? On a bedroom door?

Shaking his head, he went down the hallway to brush his teeth. He was too tired to think.

Parker gritted his teeth as he stepped upon another stone. It was maybe the size of a nickel, but to a guy with the old injuries that he had it was enough to knock him off balance, which meant pain. If he'd been smart he would have put on his boots before he came after Andy, but he doubted he would have been able to reach over to tie them.

"Come on."

Parker looked down at Andy. She'd stomped off without him earlier, but she'd come back. She motioned for him to drape his arm over her shoulders.

"No, I'm fine."

"Bullshit. You're in pain and slowing down. If you go any slower, you'll be going backwards."

Grinning at her acerbic comment he draped his left arm over her narrow shoulders. Then, as they headed up the path he found himself very thankful for her help. There were a couple of times he almost tripped. He hated not being as mobile as he used to be. It had been shocking to realize how fucked up his body was. The man who had tortured him had been a master. He would never regain what he once had.

It was also darker than sin out here. They knew they were heading in the right direction, though, because they could see the glow from the cabin.

"So, are you attached?"

He could have shot himself all over again for asking that stupid question. He knew she didn't have anyone. She never would have let him hold her if she did.

"Sorry, none of my business."

She sighed as they headed up the slope. "No. No one. Not even a cat."

Parker snorted in spite of himself. "Seems like I said something about a cat as I left, huh?"

"You did."

"I'm sorry about that, Andy. All I can say is, I was hurt and I lashed out. I'd never been in a relationship like ours and I definitely hadn't been dumped that hard before. It was a learning experience."

"I'm sorry I was so blunt," she said quietly. "I should have taken more care with my words."

"You killed me that night. Whether you realized it or not, I was never the same."

She sniffed and he wondered if she was crying. "I'm sorry. I had to protect my heart."

Yes, she was definitely crying. A long time ago, he would have loved to make her cry, to give her back some of the hurt she'd given him, but not anymore. He pulled her to a stop and cupped her face in the dim light. "It was a long time ago, Andy. I eventually understood why you did what you did, but the scar is still there. Honestly, I never expected to see you again. When my old commander called and told me you were in danger, I had this fear in my heart and I knew I had to come."

Leaning forward he pressed a kiss to her forehead, then wrapped her into his arms. For a moment she stayed firm, then she sagged into him. "I'm glad you did, Parker. Once you're rested up we'll talk about that night. I've carried a lot of guilt about it and it'll be good to clear the air. Come on, you big lug."

They completed the slow trip back to the cabin in silence. The steps took a lot out of him, but he made it. Roz looked up at them as they walked through the door. "I was about to go looking for you."

He grinned and hugged Andy to him. "I was safe."

"You better get to bed. You need to sleep to heal. I put you in the middle bedroom with the two twin beds. Mac is already in there."

Parker gave Roz a mock salute, then reluctantly pulled away from Andromeda. With another kiss to the top of her head he headed toward the hallway. "Thank you, Roz, for everything you've done."

"Yeah, yeah," she said. "Here are a couple of pain pills for when you wake up in the night."

She crossed the room and dropped two pills into his open hand. "There's a bottle of water on your bedside table."

Grinning, he blew her a kiss, though she stood only a couple of feet before him.

Parker felt fine. He'd been shot before, and the pain was excruciating but manageable. The thought of laying down was almost orgasmic.

And when he lowered himself to the narrow mattress a few minutes later, it was as good as he expected. He was asleep within seconds.

Roz caught her eye. "Why don't you get a drink and join me for a minute?"

Without a word Andromeda went into the kitchen, found a wine glass and poured herself a glass of red. Then she returned to the living room and sat down on the couch with Roz, knee bent up on the cushion. "What's up?"

"Nothing in particular. I just wanted to check on you, and your frame of mind."

Andromeda sighed. "I'm okay. I'm not gonna lie, that woman attacking me as I got off the elevator was shocking. I can't remember ever being in any kind of altercation like that. And she had a knife. I think she would have killed me and not thought a thing about it."

Roz nodded. "I have a feeling you're right. I'm glad you kicked her ass."

They sat for a few minutes, just drinking wine and talking about small things. "I need to run somewhere tomorrow and get some clothes and things."

"I'll go with you. Actually, we'll take my car just in case. Did you see the bullet holes in the back of yours?"

Andromeda looked at her sharply. "Really?"

"Yup."

That aggravated her and made her sad. She'd spent a lot of money on that car and she wasn't sure her insurance covered perforation. "It was kind of crazy in that park. I didn't even notice."

"Apparently."

Roz paused and Andromeda could tell she was building up to something. "Parker seems like a decent guy."

Andromeda laughed. "Yes. Seems to be. It shocked the hell outta me when I saw him out there fighting those guys. Total blast from the past."

"I'm sure. Any lingering feelings?"

She sighed, knowing what Roz was getting at. "I don't know. We have some things to talk about, definitely. But I'll wait until he's better and we're out of this mess."

Roz nodded her dark head and burrowed her fingers into her hair, propping her elbow on the back of the couch. "I just don't want you to get hurt again. He looks at you like he wants to eat you up."

Andromeda flushed and shifted, looking away. Maybe he did. "He wouldn't be here if he hadn't been sent. He didn't look for me for any other reason than to make sure I was safe. Apparently, someone wants me to keep doing what I'm doing."

Frowning, Roz reached out to rest a hand on her shoulder. "I just want you safe. You are so very important to me."

Andromeda's eyes watered and she leaned forward to hug her best friend. "I know I am, and you're just as important to me."

Roz laughed as she pulled back, wiping her eyes. "I know, but I'm not being chased by international terrorists and being saved by Navy SEALs."

Andromeda shook her head in exasperation. "I'm going to bed. I'm a walking zombie right now. I love you, Roz."

"I love you too, dear. Sleep soundly."

Andromeda could have wept as she crawled into the bed. This was where she normally stayed and she loved this mattress. She could feel bruised areas on her hips where she'd fallen, and her tailbone was definitely tender.

She thought about Roz's words. Her friend had a right to be concerned about Parker being back in her life. It had taken her a long time to recover after the last time, and she'd never had a relationship to equal it. They'd only been together two weeks, but it had been the most impactful two weeks of her life.

And it had fallen apart because of her.

She wasn't looking forward to talking to Parker about it.

WHEN SHE WOKE up the next morning feeling rested and restless, Roz suggested they go ahead and run down the mountain to get supplies. It was early, just after dawn.

"Parker's going to be pissed."

"He may not even notice. I checked on him early this morning and he was running a bit of a fever. I gave him more pain pills and he went back to sleep almost immediately."

Mac stood in the living room, perusing Roz's shelf of books on the far wall.

"Mac, can I get you some things?"

He looked relieved and nodded his head. "I would really appreciate it. I doubt I'll be allowed back into my apartment in the near future."

Andromeda agreed but she gave him a smile. "I'll take care of everything. If you can write down your sizes it would make it easier on me."

The big man gave her a single nod and moved to Roz's window desk, looking for pen and paper. He jotted a few things down then handed it to her. Andromeda tucked it into her pocket. "If you can watch for Parker and let him know where we went, I would appreciate it."

Mac nodded. "Of course."

Roz had already started her truck and they took off as soon as Andromeda was strapped in. It was easier going down the mountain than up, but both ways were exceptionally bumpy. By the time they reached the bottom Andromeda felt like a milkshake.

Though it was a little farther away, Roz drove them to a bigger town so that they would be a little less noticeable. They went to a Kohl's and found most of the clothes they needed, even the big and tall they needed for Mac. Then they headed to a grocery store to stock up. Andromeda even found Mac a couple of paperback books to read. By the time Roz filled up at a gas station, several hours had gone by. After making one last stop, they headed back to Roz's mountain.

Parker was standing on the front porch when they pulled up and Andromeda didn't like the expression on his face. He looked livid.

"Why didn't you tell me where you were going?"

Andromeda frowned as she circled the vehicle to the back. "Well, you were ass out asleep, which you desperately needed. No one has followed us here and we needed supplies."

One hard hand wrapped around her arm. "I'm supposed to be protecting you."

She hadn't even realized he'd come down the steps.

"No, you're supposed to be protecting him." She tipped

her chin at Mac, who had come down the steps to help them unload. "He's the linchpin in this case, not me."

Parker scowled but she could see he agreed with her.

"Here." She handed him the stack of pizzas. "Can you carry those in?"

Parker tried to stay grumpy, but it was hard. She knew he loved pizza. Especially this kind.

"Did you get a Founder's Favorite?" he growled.

"Yes."

She waited to grin until he turned back to the steps. Roz caught her eye and shook her head. "You two already sound like you're married."

That sobered Andromeda hard. They weren't like that. They never had been. She just knew things about him and ... well, she didn't know. She'd always been attracted to Parker, and the experience that life had etched onto his face looked good. It had matured him. But she knew at the heart of the matter when this was all done, they would go their separate ways again, and she would be left wanting all over again. It had taken her years to get over him.

As she looked at his broad, strong back disappearing into the cabin, she knew she needed to guard her heart. Again.

CHAPTER 11

PARKER WOULD NOT ADMIT that she'd been right, but he did feel a lot better after the twelve hours of sleep he'd gotten the night before. He was normally a fast healer and this wound would be just like the rest. Pure pain for a couple of days, then aggravation. By the third day he would be able to push it to the back of his mind.

Pizza would help, he decided, grabbing another piece. His gut was already achingly full, but the damn stuff was addictive. Andromeda had gotten hers and moved to the couch to eat it. Glancing into the room he could see she'd discarded the plate to the coffee table and now sat with a water glass in hand, talking softly to Roz. A fire had been built in the huge fireplace, radiating enough heat he felt it all the way over here. The temperature had fallen so Roz had built it up, just in case. Mac had eaten a few pieces of pizza, then immersed himself into the books Andromeda had bought him. He sat in a corner armchair, head down, flipping pages regularly.

Parker closed up the boxes and stacked them to the side.

He would eat it for dinner, too. Pizza covered every food group.

Looking back at Andromeda, he felt an emotional pang in his chest. The woman was stunning, her short hair wisping down over her forehead and her full lips spread into a smile as she talked to her best friend. Roz shot him a glance and he wondered what they were talking about, exactly. He was too far away to hear.

Pushing up from his chair, Parker crossed into the warm living room, settling onto the couch beside Andromeda. She glanced at him from the corners of her eyes. "What are we talking about?"

He could have waited for her to answer but her gaze shifted away. He glanced at Roz.

"We were just wondering where you'd been all these years."

He glanced at Andy, but she was looking down into her water glass.

"I've been all over the world. It's what a SEAL does. If there's a hotspot in the known world, we probably have a team there."

"When did you get out of the SEALs?"

"Four years ago."

"Why?"

Parker blinked, wondering if he dared tell her a bit of what happened. "I had to take a medical discharge."

Roz stared at him, waiting for more, but he didn't think he wanted to humor her, so he stared right back. She'd seen his scars and she probably had an idea what had happened. Eventually she seemed to get that he didn't want to talk about it, and the conversation turned to other things.

Parker watched Andy talk. She'd always been an eloquent woman, but with age she'd become more self-assured. It was amazing to him that she wasn't attached to someone. Or that she hadn't had kids. "Did you move on?" He asked abruptly.

A touch of color shaded her cheeks and she looked at him. "What?"

"That was what you told me to do and I was curious if you'd followed your own advice. It doesn't seem like you have."

She frowned, glancing at Roz and Mac. "I don't think this is the time for this conversation."

Quietly, Mac stood up from his chair and headed toward the bedroom hallway. "I'll be reading in my room."

Parker didn't even acknowledge him, just stared into Andromeda's eyes. "Did you?"

The silence drew out painfully.

"Andromeda, I'll stay if you want me to."

Andy glanced at Roz and shook her head. "I'll be fine. Give us a minute, Roz."

Once the two of them cleared out of the room, Andy looked back at him. "In a way, I did, yes."

"What do you mean," he demanded.

Andy rubbed her hands together. "I threw myself into my work."

"You never had another relationship?"

"I didn't say that," she said carefully. "I've had relationships over the past eight years, just not long-term ones."

"Why not?"

She shrugged defensively. "Why do you think?"

He stared at her hard, anger boiling up inside him. "I don't know why, that's why I'm asking."

She looked into the fire, her arms crossed over her chest. "I loved you, Parker. With everything I had. But I knew if I stayed with you I would be in this endless loop of euphoria and despair. When you were home things would be good, but I knew as soon as you left, my life would go to hell. The job you were doing was dangerous in the extreme and I knew it was only a matter of time before my heart was broken. I knew the longer I was with you the worse it would be, so I chose to end it early, before I became any more attached."

"You gutted me when you did that. Literally, I think a bullet through the heart would have been less painful than the shit you spewed at me."

She flushed, looking down at her hands. "You're a strong man, Parker, and determined. When you wouldn't agree to break up with me I had to get dirty. You weren't listening," she cried, looking up at him. "I tried to break it off gently, but you kept pushing and teasing and cajoling until I lashed out. I'm sorrier for that than you can imagine, but I had to. I know all of those things I said were exaggerations, but I had to get my point across."

He sagged back against the cushions of the couch. "That was harsh, Andy. I carried that shit around for months, second-guessing everything I did."

Parker could hear her voice ringing in his brain as clearly as they were talking now. He couldn't even remember what had started the fight, but he'd tried to pull her into his arms and she'd resisted.

"See, you always do this," she snapped, snatching her arm out of his grip. *"Any time I disagree with you, you manipulate me into agreeing. You do it every time you come over here. No matter what I have going in, you coax me into shoving it all aside for your benefit. My GPA has dropped a half a point because I'm not getting my work done on time, because I'm catering to you. You are the most self-centered, egotistical jock I've ever had the misfortune to meet, and I'm*

tired of it. You're spoiled, Parker. You get everything you want at the expense of everyone else."

"I don't do that," he said, feeling attacked.

She'd flung her hair back angrily. "The fuck you don't. I'll admit I was good with it for a while, but I can't cater to you every single day. You need to leave."

He remembered what he'd done then, too. Using all of his considerable charm he'd wheedled a smile out of her. A little more cajoling and apologizing and they'd been fucking on the couch. When they were done, she'd stood up from the couch and looked at him with despair in her vibrant golden eyes. "See what I mean?"

He'd left then and he hadn't returned. If Parker was honest with himself, he knew he'd manipulated her, but he'd been driven. They'd fucked from the first night they'd been together and every night after that, sometimes several times a night, and she'd been a fever in his blood that wouldn't allow him to rest.

It was hard, but he had seen what she'd meant, and he hadn't returned. The class he'd been attending had one more week in Boston, and the time there seemed to drag, knowing that he was so close to her but not allowed to be with her. If he could have left and headed back to Virginia early, he would have, but the training had been scheduled for a long time and he doubted he would be able to get it again. He'd gone back to the bar where they'd met twice but she hadn't been there. And he didn't see any of her friends, either.

Parker left a few days later, and it was like he was leaving a part of himself behind. Though she'd hurt him more than anyone else ever had, he still craved her.

When he got back to the team in Little Creek, Virginia he threw himself into training. Being a SEAL was a difficult job, and he pushed himself right to the edge. When the Lieutenant was telling you that you were going overboard and needed to chill, that was no small concern. The teams had taught him to be strong, and now he was being punished for it.

Breaking up with Andromeda had fucked him up in the head, and he had paid for it.

"I was young, Parker," she told him softly. "I'd dated, but I'd never been involved with someone as strong as you and it was a completely new dynamic. If I knew then what I know now, I think we both would have walked away with fewer scars."

Parker looked at her, wondering if she realized how offhand that comment sounded. "I was in love with you," he said simply.

Tears filled her eyes and she looked away, brushing her fingers across her cheeks. "I was in love with you, too," she whispered.

He'd almost missed those quiet words, thinking about what he was going to say next, but his brain stalled out. She'd loved him. Damn. He'd kind of suspected, but neither of them had actually said the words out loud.

That made the loss that much harder, and he felt his chest heaving, as if he'd just been struck a blow. "I'd have fought for you harder if I'd known."

She smiled sadly, looking at him sideways. "Neither one of us were ready for something that heavy. It hit us hard and fast and we didn't have the experience or maturity to know how to deal with it."

He thought of holding her in his arms down at the stream. That feeling hadn't diminished for him, and it scared him. But you didn't get anything in life if you didn't let your wants be known. Just the thought of the words he was about to utter made his cock hard. "We're older now and wiser, I hope..."

Andy turned to him, her mouth open slightly. Parker could tell he'd surprised her. Expressions of terror and surprise and softness all streaked across her face, before settling into a frown. She shook her head. "No, this is even worse. We're in a do or die situation, literally. This is not the place to rekindle a love affair gone wrong."

He shrugged lightly, though his heart shuddered in his chest. "Just thought I'd mention it."

He pushed up from the couch and hoped she didn't see the reaction of his body. Ignoring the pain in his gut, he slipped on his boots. "I'm going for a walk."

ANDROMEDA SAT IN SHOCK. Parker opened and closed the door softly behind him, and she had to wonder if he was really that calm. Last time she'd turned him down he'd gone a little crazy.

She looked down at her dark maroon t-shirt. Her nipples pressed against the fabric, hard. Her body totally remembered the feel of his body against, inside, hers. Throughout the past twelve years she'd had other lovers, but if she was honest with herself none of them had ever lived up to what Parker had been able to do with her body. He'd made her come more in those two weeks they'd been together than she ever had again, and it was a tempting offer he'd just dropped in front of her.

But they'd be in the same situation all over again. Yes, they were older and wiser, but when this job was done he would still be leaving. They lived over a thousand miles apart now, even further than they had before.

What had he been thinking, throwing that down?

The same thing she had. That he'd been the best fuck she'd ever had, and she wanted to taste it all again.

Huffing, Andromeda pushed up from the couch and headed into the kitchen for a glass of wine. So, what if it was only lunchtime?

———

Roz DIDN'T like seeing Andromeda in pain. By the time she left her bedroom to start some laundry forty minutes later, she thought she'd given them enough time. But Andromeda was alone on the kitchen. "Where did Parker go?"

Andy shrugged. "Not sure. He left about half an hour ago, after he offered to take up where we left off."

Roz stared, slipping into the chair across from her. "No way! That's ballsy. What did you say?"

"No, of course."

Roz looked at her friend sharply. "But did you mean it?"

"I don't know." Andy shook her head and when she looked up there were tears in her eyes. "I keep thinking back to when he'd been shot right in front of me. It went through my mind that 'damn, we're never going to get it right'. If I didn't care anything for him would I think that? I mean, it's been eight years. Shouldn't that be enough time to get over someone?"

Shrugging, she reached out to stroke Andy's hand. "I'm not sure. I don't have the greatest experience to speak from."

Andy dropped her head to the table. "When we were down at the stream he hugged me, and it was like the years between us were just gone. My body, well," she said, her voice muffled. "My body remembered him. I'll say that."

Uh oh. "Doesn't he live in Colorado?"

Andromeda sat up and flung out a hand. "Exactly! Even though we're eight years out, nothing has really changed. He's still doing dangerous jobs and logistically we're nowhere near each other. It's the same now as it was then."

Then she blinked, and Roz could see tears in her eyes. Her friend was really struggling, and she had no good advice to give her. Men in general set her on edge and she couldn't even imagine going to bed with one again. Yeah, sex had been good, but she could do better with the toys in her drawer when the need arose.

"So, you're smarter and wiser now, right? You will know going into anything with Parker that it's going to end. Right?"

Andy stared at her hard, obviously amazed that Roz would even consider saying 'maybe'.

"And if I fall in love again?"

She wished she could give her a good, solid answer, but Roz could only shrug. "I guess that's a choice only you can decide. You map out your risk and reward and decide which you want more."

Andy nodded, looking out the window. Did she even realize what she'd done, Roz wondered.

"This could not happen at a worse time," she whispered.

"Agreed."

Roz poured her another glass of wine, then a second one for herself. When Mac entered the room, she poured him a glass as well, then motioned to another kitchen chair.

"What are we drinking to?" he asked.

"Old flames," Roz told him.

Mac lifted his brows in surprise but didn't say anything, just swallowed his wine down. Roz liked how he just sat back and was supportive without saying much at all. He had a calm, steady peace about him that she found surprisingly welcome. "Did I hear Andy say you were a former Green Beret?"

He blinked, his gray eyes turning cautious. "I was. For almost fifteen years."

"Wow. That's really something. What made you get out of it?"

His gaze flickered, and he looked away. "I saw too many things that I didn't like, so I did what I needed to get away from it."

She could admire that. It was hard to walk away from a career after that long. "And what do you do now?"

Mac gave her a smile, the whiskers of his beard moving. "Well, I was teaching at Ohio State for a while, and now I'm taking some classes in biology. I don't have a specific path in mind. I just love learning about things."

Hm. She'd thought about going back to college herself for the same reason.

His gaze focused in on hers and he leaned forward in his chair, toward her. "And what are you doing all alone on this mountain, Rosalind White?"

He asked so softly, so coaxingly, that she answered him without thought. "Healing."

Roz blinked, realizing what she'd said, but Mac didn't push her about it. Instead he nodded and looked out the window.

"This is a good place to do it, I think."

And just that easily he accepted the reason for her crazy. When Roz felt the relief flow through her, she could have laughed. Here she was thinking she was all tough and hard and those few words made a knot of tension in her tummy ease. Had she really been that worried about it?

She glanced at Andy. The younger woman's eyes were wide, and she had a soft smile on her lips.

Mac poured himself another glass of wine. "People deal with things the way they need to."

"Yes, they do," she agreed, nodding at her glass. Mac poured her the last of the bottle.

"I'm going to go get my computer and catch up on some things," Andy murmured.

They watched as she slipped her shoes on and jogged out to the car. She came back with her messenger bag in hand and went into the living room. Within a few minutes they heard computer keys clacking.

"How awkward do you think it's going to be staying in the house with those two?" He tipped his bearded chin toward Andy.

Roz laughed, and it surprised her. A man hadn't made her laugh like that for a long time. "I don't know. We only have a day or two. It can't get too bad."

CHAPTER 12

ANDROMEDA CURSED as she read her email. Mike had sent her three.

The first was that the cop was going to be okay. He'd sustained a head injury, but it wasn't too bad. He would be okay to testify in court.

The second email was to tell her that he hadn't heard from the defendant's counsel. They had until Monday at noon to decide whether or not they were going to take the plea deal. Otherwise the trial started on Wednesday.

The third email was what made her curse. The cop recovering from the head injury had been found dead in his hospital room bathroom, apparently the victim of strangulation or poison.

Tears started in her eyes and she rested her head in her hands for a moment. Officer Tracey had been a good, true blue cop, husband and father with two small daughters. He'd been one of those guys that had gotten into police work for all the right reasons, to help people.

These terrorists were leaving a trail of destruction in their wake that would be felt for generations, and they just didn't care. Andromeda wanted to believe that everyone had a place in their beautiful country, but when terror groups took advantage and started waging war against their hosts, it was just too much. This group was in her home city and she wanted them gone.

She put a Skype call through to Mike, hoping he was in his office.

"What the hell is going on up there?" she demanded. "I thought you had him under protection?"

Mike scowled, his smoothly shaved face wrinkling. His iron gray hair looked mussed, like he'd been running his fingers through it. "We did. I had two cops on him at all times. He was being discharged and he'd gone into the bathroom to change. We're not sure how long the attacker was in there or even how he got in, we're looking at surveillance tapes now. But he killed Tracey then offed himself. We found a needle at the scene and we're testing it now."

"We look like jackasses, Mike. I'm down to one witness."

"I know, Andromeda. I don't want you to come back into town until Wednesday morning, right before court."

"You don't think he'll take the deal?"

Mike scrubbed a hand over his face. "I'm not going to hold my breath, I'll tell you that much."

Yeah, she wasn't either.

"Is your guy still good to go?"

"Yes, he is."

"Still have your SEAL protector with you?"

"Yes."

They were silent for a moment.

"I don't have to tell you to be careful," Mike said eventually. "I know you will be. Take care of that witness."

She glanced up as Mac walked into the room. "I will do my damnedest."

They hung up and Andromeda sat back with a sigh.

"How much did you hear?" she asked Mac.

"All of it."

Mac sighed as he sank down beside her on the couch. "This one is going to get hairy, isn't it?"

She nodded her head, staring into the middle distance as she thought about what she needed to do.

PARKER RAN a bucket of soapy water and begged a few rags from Roz, then went out to clean Andy's car. They were going to need it in a couple of days.

He cleaned for a solid half hour before dropping the final rag in the bloody-watered bucket. He'd known he'd lost a lot of blood, but damn. That had been a *lot*.

He left the doors open so that it would air dry and tossed out the water. He rinsed the rags at the outside spigot, but he doubted they would ever come completely clean again.

Parker went into the house and gave himself a shower next, then headed to the kitchen for leftover pizza. Roz glanced at him as she stood at the counter peeling potatoes. "Dinner will be in a couple hours."

He gave her a grin. "I know. This is just a snack."

She shook her head at him.

"Where did Andy go?"

Roz gave him a narrow-eyed look. "Not sure. Maybe she needs some alone time."

Parker sighed. "I just want to talk to her."

"I think she'd have found you if she was interested."

He tried not to let her words hurt, but they did.

"Listen, Parker. You seem like a nice enough guy, but in

two or three days you'll be gone again, and I'll be here with a bottle of wine picking up the pieces you leave behind." Her pale eyes flashed. "If I can head that heartache off at the pass I would like to do just that. Do you understand? I've seen the way you look at Andromeda. You would consume her if you could, I see that. And I realize it's not just one sided. But you are going to break her heart when you leave."

He clenched his jaw and looked out the window, not liking what he was hearing but understanding that her friendship wouldn't allow her to sit idly by as her friend walked into a potentially hurtful situation.

And she was completely right. Andromeda would never leave her job and it would be very hard for him to leave his. He'd just gotten on at Lost and Found within the past two years, and he enjoyed the people there. They all had physical issues so there was an understanding there that he would probably never find anywhere else. Not unless he created his own agency. And hired the same type of people.

"I know there's probably not much chance of anything happening between us," he told her eventually, "but I need to be sure, Roz. I know she's your friend but this attraction isn't just one-sided."

She blinked and looked down at the table. "I know, Parker. But you need to do everything in your power not to hurt her."

He gave her a sad smile. "If things go the way they did last time I'm going to be the one walking away with a hole in my chest."

ANDROMEDA KNEW HE WOULD COME.

She looked up from her computer screen to see Parker

limping down the bank to the bridge. The short dirty blond hair was dark, like he'd just taken a shower, and it looked like he'd changed clothes. He wore a pair of blue jeans today, not the black BDUs from the first day. The jeans looked good on him, though he moved like he was hurting. He wore an olive green t-shirt. Looked like something military. And his weapon was on his hip in a slide holster.

She didn't even notice the irregularity in his face anymore. She'd gotten used to it. It was just Parker, handsome as always.

The crazy part was, he moved like he was in pain, but she didn't get the feeling that it was pain from his gunshot wound.

"Are your legs hurting you?"

He blinked as he stepped up into the gazebo and sat down on the bench about a foot from her. "Saw the scars, huh?"

She looked at him askance. "Kind of hard not to. What happened?"

He clenched his jaw and she knew she shouldn't be asking. Hell, what had happened to him might be classified, but she was damn curious. It looked like someone had just started cutting on him.

"I was in Yemen on a mission that went bad. I was wounded and got captured. I was a guest of the Taliban for two days before my boys managed to find me and get me out. My interrogator was well known for his knife work, and he'd recently developed a Misery-type hammer fetish." His gray eyes darkened as he scrubbed his hands together. "I don't remember much of that week after they grabbed me and took me home, but I remember waking up when the sedative wore off and they were x-raying my legs. The bones were so broken that they looked twisted on the scans. My ankles looked like bags of marbles."

She cringed, her stomach clenching with nausea at the thought of how he'd been injured. "I'm so sorry, Parker. My god."

He shrugged nonchalantly, but she could see the pain in his eyes. "You needed to know. I'm never going to be that cocky bastard that used to carry you everywhere. I can barely carry myself through a doorway."

He gave her a look, as if considering how much to tell her.

"What?" She asked.

"I dreamt of you when I was in there. It was the only beautiful thing I had left. My mind. And the things we did together. The bastard couldn't take that away from me."

His voice got rough at the end and she could see he was fighting some strong emotion. That made her feel emotional too. She scooted closer and gripped his hand. "What did you think about?"

He gave a harsh laugh. "Everything. The way you would swing your hair over your shoulder and braid it. The way your skin glistened when you stepped out of the shower and into the towel I held for you. The way you used to ride me. And no matter what I had been out doing, as soon as you saw me you opened your arms to me. Those visions kept me sane."

"That was so long ago, though. Haven't you had other relationships?"

Parker immediately shook his head. "I've had hookups not relationships. Those two weeks we had together are the most vivid two weeks of my life. The memories of our time together got me through torture in Yemen, and the pain of recovery, which was almost as bad. I have to thank you for that."

Lifting her hand, he pressed a kiss to the back of it, then let it rest on his thigh. "I did a lot of things wrong back then, but I want you to know that I loved you with all my heart. Yeah, I know I didn't have the maturity I needed to, but I did have the emotion."

Andromeda blinked, her eyes suddenly awash in tears. "Thank you for telling me that, Parker. I loved you too, but you scared me. Everything was so carefree and fun, and you made me forget all about the plans for the rest of my life. If you had asked me to run away with you I probably would have."

He looked at her in surprise. "Really? Wow," he breathed. "What a tempting idea. The government would have been on my ass, though."

They chuckled together, and she leaned more into his shoulder. "I wish things had turned out differently."

"I do too, Andy."

They sat like that for a long time, listening to the water in the stream and the sound of each other's breathing. It was the most relaxed she could remember being for the past two days. No, the past week. Parker had matured over the years and she appreciated that.

That maturity had come at a price though. She couldn't imagine the torture he'd gone through to receive the scars he had. It had to have been horrendous. What kind of person would do that?

The same type that would try to kill children at an art fair.

"What are we going to do?" She asked quietly.

"Well," he heaved a heavy breath, his shoulder moving against her own. "We're going to get back to Ohio and you will win your court case. Are you sure this guy won't take the plea deal?"

Andromeda shook her head. "I don't think so. They're so loyal to each other and their cause, I doubt that he's even considered it."

Parker was quiet for a long time. "What are the details of the plea deal, can I ask?"

Andromeda gave him an outline of what they were asking for. Mozi had tried to carry out a lone wolf attack and he'd completely screwed it up. She knew he would not name his father as one of the planners of that attack. But the Christmas parade, on the other hand, was a different story and he just might. That had been a successful attack in their opinion and worthy of praise.

Andromeda thought that Mozi's father was trying to protect him, even though he was only a fourth or fifth son. The direct witnesses at the art fair crime scene, other than Mac, were all dead, but they still had security footage of Mozi in the truck. All of the effort the al Fareq family was going to in order to extinguish the witnesses was in vain.

Something hit her then. "I wonder... if I let it be known that we have footage of Mozi in the truck, I wonder if his family would back down."

"That is an excellent thought," Parker told her. "It's not public knowledge?"

She shook her head. "We released a generic clip of the truck, but not the one of him getting out of the truck with a gun in hand."

Andromeda tapped a finger to her lips. "I need to call Mike and have him put out a press release."

Turning to Parker, she leaned up and gave him a kiss on the corner of his mouth. "Thank you for making me talk about this. I think if the family will disavow him, he'll retaliate by taking the plea deal. Oh, this could be good."

She turned away, then immediately spun back. "Thank you for telling me about Yemen. I know it wasn't easy."

Pressing another kiss to his cheek, she looked at him for a long moment. Without another word she left the gazebo and jogged up the hill to the cabin.

Mike was surprised by her call but seemed excited about her plan. "Let me make a few calls and see if I can pull a few strings at the Columbus Dispatch. We might be able to make this work."

Andromeda waited for a while, then started pacing. When Roz asked her what was going on she explained.

"Oh, that's a good idea. I hope it works."

Less than an hour later Mike returned her call. "My contact said she would be more than happy to do up a little article for us and sprinkle in some key details. It will be front page in tomorrow's Dispatch and featured on all their social media accounts."

"No way," Andromeda breathed. "Oh, that makes me very happy. If we play this right his family could completely disavow him. Will his attorney see this article?"

"Oh, I'm sure. Pete Mancuso gets his coffee and paper every morning at one coffee shop. I know for a fact he'll see it."

"Did Mozi tell his family they had him on tape?"

"I seriously doubt it. I don't think they realize how much evidence we have against him. If they did, they wouldn't have tried to get rid of all the witnesses. This is a good plan, Andromeda."

She laughed lightly. "I had help working this out."

"Stay near your phone. Hopefully I'll have some good news for you tomorrow."

"Okay. Later, Mike."

PARKER DROWSED on the padded bench for a while before moving to the couch thing. He worried that he would be too big for it, but it actually was very sturdy. And damn comfortable. He felt safe enough that when his lids drifted shut he allowed himself to relax and drift off to sleep.

"Parker Quinn."

For a moment he was disoriented, but when he looked up into Andy's smiling face he knew he was okay, wherever he was. She grinned down at him, then leaned down to press a kiss to his lips. Without hesitation he cupped her head in his hands and kept her mouth on his own, tasting her, remembering her. If she had shown the slightest hesitation he would have let her go, but she didn't.

"Oh, Andy," he whispered. "You feel like home to me."

Blinking, she looked down at him in surprise. "What?"

"You taste just so much better than I remember. And I feel like we belong together. This feels right."

Bracing a hand on the back of the divan, she leaned down to kiss him again, tilting her head to lick at the seam of his lips. Parker cupped her waist, then her ribcage and her shoulders in his hands, rubbing them up and down.

When she pulled back, he let her go. He didn't want her to feel pressured in any way.

"Dinner is ready, if you're hungry. If you're comfortable I'll let you sleep but you've been down here for several hours."

He shook his head. "No, I'm good. I was just sitting in the sun and being warm and the next thing I know you're waking me up."

She grinned at him. "You were pretty cute laying there, your mouth hanging open and snoring."

He scowled at her even as he shifted up to a sitting position. "Whatever," he laughed.

"You were! I heard you as I was walking down the trail."

Embarrassment warmed his cheeks and he hoped she was exaggerating. He never used to snore. It was a safety issue for SEALs. It had been too long since he'd left the teams.

They walked back up the hill together and the mood was definitely lighter. Parker was feeling better in general and Andy's mood had improved after talking to her boss about the plan to release info. "It would definitely be nice to get to the courthouse without having to run a gamut of bullets and people trying to kill us," he murmured.

Andy wrapped her arm through his elbow and he couldn't decide if she'd done it for him or for her. He appreciated the balance she gave him, but he didn't want her treating him like he needed help. That was one of the most aggravating things about the injuries he'd received in Yemen. They were visible, and people tended to treat him like he was less of a man.

Even if he was, in fact, less physically capable than the man he'd been, he didn't want other people treating him like it.

She didn't say anything, though, so he chose to believe that she just wanted to touch him as they walked up the slope together.

Mac and Roz were at the table eating dinner already. It looked like Roz had made pork chops, potatoes, and buttered corn. Some of her phenomenal biscuits were in a basket in the middle of the table. After settling Andy into a seat he took his own chair.

After they'd taken the edge off their hunger, they started talking about inconsequential things and he realized sitting there that he enjoyed all of these people. Roz was a little prickly about things, but he could understand why with her background. Mac took the middle of the road in everything just to keep from getting into an argument. He listened to everyone's opinions or positions and managed to state his position calmly, using neutral language without animosity or heat. Parker appreciated that because it was so easy to spew anger at people these days, or to try to force your opinion on other people. That was the entire reason they were in this situation. The al Fareq family had tried to force their opinion on the community that housed them. And now the community was fighting back.

Parker hoped that Mozi would take the plea deal. It was good for everyone involved. Well, except for the Fareq family. That wasn't his concern. Getting them off the streets was.

Andromeda's phone pinged with an incoming email. She swiped a few times, then sat back in the chair to read. "Oh, damn this is good. They did it. It'll be in the morning paper."

Parker reached over and squeezed her hand. "That's excellent."

"Now to hope they take the bait and cut him off," Mac murmured.

They all looked down at their plates, hoping.

———

ANDROMEDA'S PHONE pinged with an incoming text message super early that morning. Mike had sent her a link to the actual article. Sitting up in her dark room she paged though the document, excitement brewing in her. This was fabulous. The details the woman had released were subtle yet worded in a way to bring attention to the fresh information. She'd done an excellent job.

Too excited to go back to sleep, Andromeda headed out to the kitchen for a glass of water. When she passed through the living room she realized there was a shape sitting in the darkness.

"Parker?"

Crossing the room, she lowered herself to the cushion beside him. Sitting up with his head in his hands, he glanced at her.

"Hey. What are you doing up?"

Andromeda looked at him in the meager light. His hair was mussed and his eyes seemed a little dazed.

"Mike sent me a link to the article," she told him. "It's incredible. I hope it does what I need it to."

"Good, good," he said softly.

Then he looked into the coals of the fire again.

"Are you okay?"

Reaching out, she rested a hand on his back and gasped. His t-shirt was wet with sweat. "Are you okay? Do you have a fever?"

She reached up to press her fingers to his forehead, but he captured her hand and folded it into his own. "No fever. Just... well, I have dreams sometimes. Flashbacks. They wake me up."

Her heart swelled with empathy for him. "I'm sorry, Parker. I can't imagine living through what you did."

He shook his head. "You know, we're trained for exactly the thing I dealt with, but it's very different when it actually happens to you for real. They don't tell you that your tormentors will go home with you, or that there's no magic pill that will make all your demons go away. They don't tell you about the aftermath. There are times that I wake up swinging and fighting... and I worry about even being in a relationship. How would I feel if we developed a relation-ship and you woke up at night with me punching you? I think hurting you would damage me even more than anything else I've been through. I would never do that to you."

Andromeda felt like her heart was going to shatter in pain. How had he dealt with this?

"How long ago did this happen to you?"

He sighed. "It's been almost four years. I got out of the Navy at thirty-one."

She shook her head. "That is so young. You gave so much to them."

Blinking, he looked back at the coals. "Yeah," he sighed. "But it was worth it. I'd do anything for the guys in my team. They literally carried me out."

"I'm sure."

She wanted to be there for him now, but she wasn't sure how. They were in such a chaotic situation right now that they barely knew what was going to happen minute to minute, let alone a week from now.

It worried her that he didn't have anyone. It sounded like his parents were gone a lot of the time and when they were home, Pennsylvania was a long way from Denver.

"And what about the people you work with now?"

His frown faded and he gave her a smile. "I haven't been there very long, but the guys are all incredible. The boss is amazing, the jobs are amazing. They don't make more out of our disabilities than we have to. If something doesn't work, we figure out a different way to do it, we adapt and overcome obstacles. I feel more useful now than

I have in a long time. I actually feel like I have a career again."

That was good. Everyone needed that kind of fulfillment.

"That's invaluable."

"Yes," he agreed softly, but there was a hesitation in his voice.

"What, Parker?"

"Nothing." He squeezed her hand again. "Thank you for checking on me. You should probably go back to bed. We still have a couple of hours before dawn."

"Why don't you come lay down with me?"

Andromeda blinked, wondering where that had come from. It hadn't been an offer she'd actually thought about issuing. It had just fallen out of her mouth.

Parker seemed too lonely sitting on the couch here in the dark.

His eyes glinted in the light from the banked fireplace. "I don't know that that would be a good idea. I already know I'm going to have a hard time giving you up again."

Damn. He really was breaking her heart.

"Come on. I just want you to hold me again like you used to. I know you're worried about hurting me, but I don't think it's as big of an issue as you think. You would never hurt me, Parker."

He cleared his throat and swallowed hard enough that she could hear, but he seemed unable to tell her no as she stood and held her hand out to him. He followed her into her bedroom and watched as she closed the door. She was wearing the t-shirt and sleep pants she'd bought at the store, conscious that there were other people in the house. Now she pulled the blankets back on the bed and motioned for Parker to crawl in. Moving gingerly, he lowered himself to the edge of her mattress and reclined, holding his side. Once he was settled she crawled in beside him and pulled the blankets over both of them. Then she stretched her arm across his belly and nestled her head against the cup of his shoulder. Immediately his arms went around her, and they both sighed. There was a little bit of light from the connecting bathroom, just enough to see.

"I never thought I'd feel this again," Parker murmured to her. "When my former commander called and told me you were on something hot, I didn't know what I was getting into, but I knew I couldn't leave you in danger."

"I can't tell you how happy I was to see you. Shocked, but happy."

He tightened his arm around her back and she felt him bury his nose in her hair.

"I love this cut on you," he murmured. "And you smell like peaches."

"Thank you. Cheap shampoo from a box store," she laughed. "And I've had this cut for a few years."

"Mm."

Andromeda's eyes were getting heavy, but she didn't want to fall asleep just yet. It had been so long since she'd held him in her arms. Parker was a big, earthy man and she loved feeling the play of muscles under his skin, and the feel of the hair on his arms tickling her arm. Her fingers started to move, just drawing lazy circles on his belly above the t-shirt fabric. Then, somehow, her fingers found bare skin.

It was like they'd both hit a live wire. Her fingers stilled, as did his breathing.

"This is dangerous," he whispered.

Yes, it was, but Andromeda couldn't imagine peeling herself away from him now.

Moving up onto an elbow she looked down into his

eyes. Parker looked resigned and worried, but a little excited too. Andromeda pushed the blankets down until she could expose his lean torso, then she pulled the t-shirt up a bit. Running her fingers over his skin, she watched the muscles tighten in response to her touch.

"Ouch," he whispered.

"Oh, sorry."

Moving away from his abdomen she pushed his shirt higher, up over his pecs. In the weak light from the bathroom she could see light striations on his skin. Scars from the torturer in Yemen. Leaning down she pressed a kiss to one of the deeper ones, then moved to another one. Parker sighed beneath her and she could feel the thud of his heart accelerate. She pressed another kiss to the flat disk of his nipple, but she was surprised when he caught her hand.

"This is going in a really dangerous direction. As much as I would love to make love with you, I don't know that now is a good time, for several different reasons."

She sighed, knowing that he was right but hating to admit it. Just that little bit of touching had warmed her body. "I know. I just kind of lost myself there for a minute."

"Let's revisit this in a few days, after the court case. I don't have to get back to Colorado right away."

Nodding, she pulled his shirt back down and nestled back into his chest. Then she pulled the blankets up again. She would have to make do with just cuddling tonight.

The fact that she'd been ready to jump his bones kind of shocked her. She hadn't slept with a man for several years, not since that junior partner from a local law firm had taken her to a Christmas party. He'd been smart and ambitious, but they'd had differing opinions on too many things. Jason had been at least five years ago.

Five? Damn. Maybe that was why her body had woken so quickly. She was in a hell of a dry spell.

Parker was right, though. Now wasn't the time or the place, as much as she hated to admit it.

Once they settled down, they slept like children, curled around each other for comfort.

Roz GAVE him a frown as he walked out of Andy's room the next morning and he couldn't help but grin. "I didn't do it," he said as she swatted him with a dishtowel. Mac looked up, a considering smile on his face as he coated a stack of pancakes with syrup. Andy came out of the room right behind him.

"Be nice, Roz. All we did was sleep."

She scowled at Andy but just shook her head. "You're old enough to know what you're doing."

Parker held a chair out for Andy to sit down, then started helping himself to the pancakes and bacon. He groaned as he stuffed a strip of meaty, salty goodness into his mouth. "Roz, you're wasted up here on this mountain."

She laughed as she sat down with her cup of coffee. "I don't think so. I'm happy in my own little world up here."

"I love it as well," Mac said softly. "The silence is golden."

Parker was surprised when Roz grinned at the big man and nodded her head. Mac seemed just as surprised, but he grinned back at her, then tucked into his pancakes.

Parker was very aware that Andy watched him almost constantly. He looked up, catching her eye, and gave her a smile. In the yellow morning light she looked soft and sexable, her hair hanging over her forehead and her skin free of makeup.

She'd held onto him the entire night last night, and he'd woken several times slightly alarmed. But as soon as he remembered who he was holding he would relax and fall back to sleep. She was such a wonderful armful.

It had been one of the hardest things he'd ever had to do to turn her down last night, but there was no way he was up to performing the way he wanted to with her. There was more work that needed to be done on their relationship, or connection... *whatever* it was right now.

And he needed to think about what he wanted if they did move forward. They had always been compatible sexually, but what would happen long term? They were each in careers that they loved. She'd invested her entire professional future in the Columbus Prosecutor's office. No, he hadn't been at Lost and Found as long, but he'd found the same camaraderie and brotherhood that he'd had in the Navy. That was invaluable to him.

He had a lot of thinking to do. What he knew right now was that it would be very easy to fall in love with her again. If he hadn't already...

CHAPTER 13

Since Roz had cooked, Andromeda washed the dishes and Parker dried and put them away, with her direction. They worked quietly together, not needing to say anything to be connected.

Occasionally Parker's hand would brush against her own as she handed him dishes and it was comforting. She'd never lived with a man before, but she could see doing it with Parker.

After all of the breakfast things were cleaned up, Roz sat him down at the table with her medical supplies. Parker shrugged out of his t-shirt, and Andromeda had to stare. Now that she knew how he had gotten all of the scars scattered across his body, she wanted to scream at the world that it wasn't right.

"Did they get the fucker?" Andromeda asked, unable to help herself.

Parker grinned at her. "My buddy Cicero did. Then he gave me the knife he'd made all these cuts with."

"Ew. That's kind of macabre."

"It was satisfaction for me," he said softly.

She rested her hand on his shoulder as Roz peeled the bandage away.

"This is looking good, Parker. I'll cover it with a water-proof bandage, then a heavier bandage. Both entrance and exit wounds look good, but you need to keep them clean, and dry preferably. If it had been any deeper it would have hit something vital, but you lucked out."

He nodded, sitting straight as she reapplied the bandages.

Andromeda's phone rang as they were finishing up. She glanced at the clock on the wall. Eleven a.m. Her heart raced when she saw who was calling.

"You'd better have good news for me, Mike."

"The ink is still wet on the paper, this sucker is so fresh."

"He signed it?" She asked incredulously. "I can't believe it."

"The jail is getting me a transcript of the conversation Mozi had with his father early this morning. I hear there was a lot of yelling. When can you be here?"

Andromeda blinked. "It will take me a few hours to get there. I'll leave within the next half hour."

"Not as quick as I would like, but I won't take this from you. I think you need to be the one to take his statement."

Damn, he was an awesome boss. "Thank you, Mike. I'll be there as soon as I possibly can."

"You better be."

They hung up and she looked at Parker, standing in the kitchen doorway. His black t-shirt was back on and he stood ready. "I'll pack my bag."

Andromeda looked at Roz. "I know we've crashed your life this week, but I need another favor."

"Name it. This is the most excitement I've had for months."

"Just in case this deal falls through somehow, could you possibly drive Mac up to Columbus for me?"

She nodded without even a hesitation. "Of course. The truck is gassed up and I'll pack a small bag now."

Andromeda crossed the room to wrap her friend in a hug. "You are an incredibly great friend. I love you to pieces."

Roz smiled and kissed her cheek. "I love you too, dear. Now get your butt moving. Can't keep the criminals waiting."

Andromeda didn't wait any longer. She went into her bedroom and packed the few things she'd accumulated. She wore a pair of jeans and sneakers right now, and it would have to do until she got to her office. She had a spare outfit there.

"Mind if I drive?"

She looked at Parker in surprise. "Sure, you feel up to it?"

He nodded firmly and she handed him the keyring. He'd changed back into a black t-shirt and BDUs. Roz must have been able to get all the blood out of them. There was a weapon strapped to his hip, and he moved more confidently than she'd seen him move in days.

Andromeda gave Parker a few directions then they were cruising north on Interstate 77. While he drove, she planned; typing out a document full of questions on her laptop. Every variation, every contingency she could think of, she made note of. She wanted these cases to be air tight.

After an hour and a half of driving, they merged onto the ramp for 70 Westbound.

"I'm going to stop and get gas."

Andromeda blinked as she put her computer away. "Yeah, I can stand to use the bathroom. Maybe we can grab some lunch too. I have a feeling that once I get in there I won't take a break for several hours."

They refueled and refreshed, then were back on the road within just a few minutes. Parker ate several sandwiches and seemed to be almost fully recovered from his gunshot wound. He was amazing. She had offered to drive but he'd waved her off. "You have work to do. I'm fine to drive. We're only about an hour and a half from Columbus, so you'd better maximize the time I'm giving you."

"Yes, sir," she laughed, pulling her computer out again.

The next time she looked up they were getting off on the Fourth Street exit and heading toward the prosecuting attorney's office. It was a Monday afternoon and things were still hopping, but no one had parked in her parking spot. She glanced at him as they got out of the car. "Um."

Parker seemed to anticipate what she was going to say. "I'm sticking with you. It's that easy. You've had two attempts on your life. You might want me to stay here but it's not going to happen that way, so get used to it."

Andromeda grinned slightly, loving this flash of ego. "I didn't think you would listen, but I had to try. Come on."

The guards at the security checkpoint gave her a funny look as she walked in, and she realized they'd never seen her in anything but a business suit. She pulled her ID tag from her messenger bag. "You can see who I am. And he's with me. Give him a visitor tag."

They did as they were told and didn't even blink as his weapon set off the metal detector. Parker held his arms up obligingly for the scanner, then moved on when they waved him through. Andromeda was impressed with the extra steps the security people were taking right now. All of the recent deaths had to be setting people on edge.

She received more second glances, then third glances as

they turned to look at her shadow in black. Leading him down a hallway, she unlocked her office and stepped inside, then relocked the door. Parker looked at her curiously.

"I have a change of clothes here."

Crossing to the coat rack in the corner she grabbed a plastic wrapped hanger. "I'm sorry. Can you turn around?"

Parker lifted his brows in surprise. "Really? It's not like I haven't seen your delectable body before."

Andromeda laughed lightly, then shrugged. "Okay."

Shrugging off her shirt, she tossed it across a chair in the corner. She wore a nice pink lace bra. It cupped her breasts like it was supposed to, but still gave her room to move. Parker huffed out a breath and she had to hide a smile. This was what he'd wanted.

Andromeda removed the blouse from the hanger and slipped it on. The bra was too dark for the cream-colored blouse, but it would have to do. She would keep her jacket on over top of it.

Turning, she pushed her jeans over her hips and tossed them in the direction of the discarded t-shirt. Then she pulled the black pants from the hangar and slipped them on. Yeah, so maybe she took her time... a little. A few extra seconds teasing Parker wasn't going to make a difference in the day.

Within just a couple of minutes she had her armor on and was ready to walk into war. Grabbing up her computer bag, she stopped in front of Parker. Without a word she went up on tiptoes to press a kiss to his lips, then let herself out of her office.

Mike was in his own office. She knocked on the door-jamb but the man behind the desk was a little busy. He waved her in and to a chair in front of his desk. Even as he continued to talk to the person on the other end of the line, his gaze tracked Parker as he entered the room behind her. Then he looked back at Andromeda.

"I don't think that's going to work, but I'll let you know."

He hung up the phone, then pulled a sheaf of papers from a stack at his right. He handed them to her.

Andromeda looked at the two-page transcript from the phone conversation. Surely they knew they were monitored while they were in jail? Even when they spoke Farsi, there was an interpreter on duty. When things had started heating up around their city, the county government considered it a necessary expense to hire an interpreter for things exactly like this.

"Oh. Parker Quinn, this is my boss, Mike Maddox."

Neither of the men moved to shake hands, which she thought was a little curious, but she didn't push it. Her eyes continued to scan the words.

'Did you read the paper this morning?'

'No.'

'Seems like there is more evidence that the police have. If you had completed your task like you were supposed to, they never would have seen your face and we could have disavowed your actions. Dalir lived up to his name. He was brave and completed the task given him. He honored our family name. You are threatening that.'

'My apologies, Father. I only wanted...'

'I don't care what you wanted. It only matters that we honor the State. You acted rashly and without family support. Now you will deal with the consequences. Whatever happens to you happens. I disavow you.'

'No, Father. Wait!'

'No, Mozi. You have had many chances to honor the family like your brothers have, but instead you persist in behaving like a lazy asshole, looking for the easy way to do

*things. You have shamed us too many times. If you have any
respect for us at all, you will take yourself from this earth.'*

'*Father!*'

'*I am not your father any longer, you cursed child. We
will continue our campaign against the infidels without you.*'

'*Father! No!*'

END OF CALL

ANDROMEDA LOOKED UP AT MIKE, excitement vibrating
through her as she handed the sheaf of papers to Parker to
read. "This is perfect! Where is he? I want to talk to him. He
waived his right to further counsel, correct?"

Mike nodded. "He did. After Mozi signed the plea
agreement, he told his counsel to leave, and he's been in the
interview room cooling his heels since then, waiting
for you."

Andromeda stood up. Parker handed her the transcript
back and she arranged it into her messenger bag next to her
computer. "Did you run Dalir al Fareq?"

Mike handed her another set of papers. "Supposedly as
clean as his brother. But it sounds like he may have been the
one driving at the Christmas parade."

"Yes, that makes sense."

She looked up at Parker, and he gave her a grin and a
nod. As the three of them walked down the hallway to the
interview room, she tried to order her thoughts. Even
though his family had disavowed him, he might still try to
protect them, unless she could make him so angry that he
chose the opposite path.

CHAPTER 14

BEFORE SHE OPENED the door Andromeda took in a long breath. Her heart was thumping with excitement because she had been working toward this for months. So much was riding on this interview.

"You'll have to wait out here," Mike told Parker.

"Not happening." Parker told him flatly. "I don't care what you say. She," he pointed a finger at Andromeda, "is not going in there without protection."

"I'll be with her," Mike said placatingly.

Parker gave him a long up and down look and crossed his arms. "Exactly."

Oh, shit!

"You two need to quit. I don't need this right now." She looked at Mike. "Parker goes in with me."

His expression coldly furious, Mike nodded once in agreement. "Fine. It's your call. If he breaks his muzzle it's on you."

Grinning, Parker leaned in and snapped his strong white teeth at Mike, making the other man jump back. Andromeda would have laughed if it wouldn't have been mean to Mike. *This* was the Parker she remembered from years ago.

PARKER STEPPED into the room and scanned every square inch. It had a decent view of the Scioto River and concrete, and that was it. He doubted the young man handcuffed to the table cared about the view, though. Crossing to the man Parker pulled his chair away from his ass and stood him on his feet, then started to search him. The man was cranked over the table and started cursing, but Parker continued. He found what he was looking for in the bottom hem of the tan jail uniform shirt. Working the small hard thing with his fingers, he pulled it from the fabric. A paperclip had been straightened and inserted into the heavier hem fabric, camouflaging it. Parker handed the modified clip to Mike, then continued to search. He found a second, similarly bent piece of metal in the hem of the white t-shirt he wore beneath the tan, this time in the back hem. He handed that one to Mike as well.

The prosecuting attorney glared, but not necessarily at him. "Two of them?"

"One in front and one in back, useful for either way he's cuffed."

Parker 'helped' the gentleman back into his chair and scooted him tight to the table, then stood back one foot and off to the side just a bit. He had a perfect view of every move the man could make.

Andromeda, looking beautiful and strong, sat across the table from Mozi and began removing papers and her computer from her bag. There was a raised electronic bank in the center of the table and she flipped a couple of switches.

"Thank you for choosing to speak to me, Mr. al Fareq. I know this hasn't been an easy process for you. I'm sure you remember my name is Andromeda Pierce. I've been prosecuting your case. And this is Mr. Michael Maddox, lead prosecutor."

Mozi muttered something under his breath and Andromeda looked at him, then down at her notes. "Now, since you've waived your right to further counsel, do you consent to speak to us without representation?"

The young man glared at her but didn't say anything.

Andromeda smiled patiently, unruffled. "Mr. al Fareq, you have to agree or disagree verbally. This conversation is being recorded."

"Yes," he hissed. "I consent, *jendeh*."

Parker's anger spiked as the punk called her a slut, but Andromeda didn't even blink, just continued to unpack her bag. Finally, she set a pen on top of a legal pad and smiled. "Now, then. I know you're very angry right now, but you really are doing the right thing. If we had gone to court you would have been even more publicly humiliated than you already are. I mean, I appreciate that you were trying to honor your family and the Islamic State by pulling off the attack on the art fair, but even you have to admit it was pretty lame. I mean, did you think that you and the bomb you put together would actually blow up? Our techs looked at it and the timer wasn't even wired into the explosive. Were you aware of that?"

"*Kiram too un dahane sag gaaeedat.*"

Fuck your dog raped mouth. That was a good insult, Parker thought, but not in relation to his woman.

He glanced at Andromeda, but she gave him the tiniest shake of her head.

"Mr. al Fareq can insult me all he wants, if that's what he just did. It's not going to change the fact that he fucked up and his family has washed their hands of him." She looked directly at Mozi. "Doesn't that piss you off that you are basically giving your life for a family that won't even recognize you? Why are you protecting them?"

"You have no concept of honor," the young man snapped.

"Mm," Andromeda looked down at her notes. "But I bet your brother did. Dalir. He was the one that drove the truck in the Christmas Parade, wasn't he?"

Mozi glared at her, disgust curling his lips. His dark eyes blazed with fury. "Yes, *kusi*, and he will be blessed beyond measure for ridding the earth of unbelievers and supporting the Islamic State."

Andromeda frowned, tilting her head. "Those children were noncombatants, which makes your brother's actions an insult to Allah."

Mozi rattled his cuffs against the metal loop they were connected to in the center of the table. "They don't matter. They were part of the coalition fighting the Islamic State. My brother will be blessed, and I will be blessed. We are doing as we are commanded."

"How will you be blessed, Mozi?"

He clamped his lips and looked out the window, anger sitting heavily upon his young brow.

Parker looked at Andromeda. She was in her element. There was an excited light in her eyes that couldn't be tamped down.

"So, what were you plans when you drove the truck through the crowd, Mozi?"

"I wanted to kill as many people as I could, because they are enemies of the Islamic State."

Andromeda gave him a condescending smile, and her expression turned sympathetic. "Ah, but you didn't, did you? You completely botched your lone wolf attack. And you got taken down by a lowly security guard, a mall cop. Isn't that embarrassing? Will ISIS disavow you as well as your family?"

Parker actually heard the young man's teeth grinding in his mouth, but he didn't say anything. But Andromeda didn't seem bothered.

"So, let's get down to brass tacks, Mozi. Your plea agreement stipulates that you will name your co-conspirators, and those of the Christmas Parade attack. So let's get to it. Your brother Dalir carried out the attack on the Christmas parade, but who planned it?"

"We all planned it. There is shared glory in a goal achieved, and we wanted to kill as many Americans as we could."

"So your father supports ISIS as well, and your mother. What about your three sisters, and the rest of your brothers?"

He shook his head. "We will all be blessed. You Americans have no chance against us, because we will attack you when and where we want. We are all soldiers and we will sow terror."

Andromeda leaned forward, intent. "But will they remember your name? Will the Islamic State remember you as a nameless bumbler who screwed up an easy job? If you give me the names of your co-conspirators, only *then* you will receive the glory you deserve, because you will be standing up for what you believe in. And you will bring them glory because they've fought their fight. They will be given credit for the attack on the Christmas parade that killed so many."

That seemed to make Mozi think. Parker had to admire Andromeda's craftiness.

"Your family members will be recognized as fighting for the Islamic State," she told him. "That's what you want, right?"

He blinked, and when Mozi looked down at his hand, Parker knew she had him. Andromeda began to list names. Parker recognized the names of Mozi's family. When Mozi answered yes to every name, she nodded. "These are your co-conspirators in the attack that killed nine children, correct?"

"Yes."

"And who of them helped you plan the art fair attack?"

"Ibrahim, my younger brother. We walked the path I was to drive the week before but there were barriers put in the way I was going to go. I had to work around them."

With the Islamic State encouraging truck and semi attacks against pedestrians, many cities had adopted the practice of placing concrete barriers at venue entrances and exits to keep people safe. Parker was sure, though, that they would come up with some other devious way to kill innocent civilians.

It took them an hour to interview Mozi, but at the end of that time they had a list of fifteen people. As well as the incredibly important addresses. Now they knew *where* they were.

"Mozi, they will talk about you in videos and on Bayan."

Mozi's eyes lit with a fanatic heat at the mention of the Islamic State radio station, and he nodded his head.

The three of them left the room after that and Mike called a deputy to transport Mozi back to jail. "I've already called the jail administrator and they're going to place him in Administrative Segregation for his own protection until he's shipped out to prison, which should be within the next few days. The judge has already signed off on the plea deal."

Andromeda nodded, then looked at Parker. "Thank you for not stepping in when he was insulting me. I've been called worse than a whore or slut before. I didn't catch the other one, though. Something about a dog?"

Parker looked at her, brow raised. She'd known what he'd said? "I'd rather not repeat it."

She smiled slightly and nodded.

It didn't surprise Parker that she'd understood some of the language. Andromeda had a passion for her job that would make her acquaint herself with every aspect of a case. She wouldn't allow a language barrier to impede her progress.

When they returned to Mike's office he made a copy of the list of names and addresses Mozi had given them. "I already notified both Columbus PD and Franklin County that we might need their SWAT teams to execute warrants. I'll call Judge Aviano and get warrants on these people within the hour. Hopefully, if the al Fareq family is as bright as the son, they'll stay exactly where they are and just wait for us to come get them."

Andromeda laughed. "Somehow I doubt it will be that easy."

CHAPTER 15

They had warrants in hand within thirty minutes, and after a joint planning meeting with the sheriff's office and the PD, multiple teams went out to serve the warrants and bring Mozi's conspirators in. Parker watched the men plan and offered a few pertinent suggestions, which were received and implemented. Once they realized he'd been a SEAL doing insertions just like this for so many years, and that he spoke several different dialects of Middle Eastern languages, they asked him to ride along.

He said yes without a moment of hesitation, then snapped his mouth shut so that he didn't let out a mighty yell of excitement. It had been years since he'd been in on a plan like this, and in spite of the amount of pain he was in, he was going to go.

Andromeda gave him a conspiratorial smile, as if she knew he felt like a kid that had just been told he was going to Disney World. He leaned over to whisper in her ear. "Where can you go while I'm doing this?"

"I'll go to my condo. Roz and Mac are there waiting for me. The people that attacked me in the garage couldn't get onto the elevator because they didn't have a resident's card. Once I'm in my condo I'll be fine."

Parker nodded. "You're probably right."

"Besides," she continued. "Mike had the chief put officers on my building."

Okay, that made him feel a lot better about the situation. As excited as he was about being invited into the SWAT command vehicle while the warrants were being served, he didn't lose sight of the fact that Andromeda was his priority. Since Mozi had taken the plea agreement, they would no longer need Mac to testify in court against him. It was smart for Andromeda to keep him close, though, just in case.

She looked up at him, her big golden eyes concerned. Even without makeup she was beautiful to him, and the worry in those eyes for *him* made his feel... humble.

"I suggest that you take one of those pain pills Roz gave you before you go out. It's hard to tell what you'll get into."

Parker loved that she was comfortable with him doing this. He was a long ways from running raids like he used to, but it was satisfying to be included even in a peripheral way. If he could help the SWAT teams with communication, he absolutely would. And it would keep up his end of the deal with Lambert. He would be exposing this sleeper cell of terrorists and putting them out of business.

ANDROMEDA WANTED to kiss Parker before she left the conference room with all the bigwigs in it, but she didn't think that would be a smart move. Parker looked like such a badass in his black BDUs and t-shirt, and sidearm, the muscles in his crossed arms bulging. She bet he had more weapons on him she didn't see, too, but no one had said a single word about him being there. Actually, they all seemed to appreciate having an expert sit in on what they were doing. When she stepped out the door he was talking about tactics that had worked for his team when they were in the field.

Just at the last minute he glanced up, smiled and gave her a wave, and that meant as much to her as a kiss. Even in the midst of his excitement he acknowledged her.

Andromeda went to her office and grabbed her clothes, stuffing them into a spare bag. Then she headed down to her vehicle. The place was crawling with cops right now, so she felt very secure walking through the parking garage. When she got to her own condo building, a CPD officer met her in the garage and walked her to the elevator. She swiped her card and greeted Hampton on the monitor when she got inside.

"It's been a little crazy around here, Ms. Pierce. Your guests arrived safely and are in your condo. If you'd like to order out just let me know and I'll make sure the food arrives safely."

Andromeda laughed. "Thank you, Hampton."

Maybe she ate out too much if the security guard was anticipating her dinner.

When she let herself into the condo, she was greeted by warm, spicy smells and Roz walking down the hallway toward her. Andromeda wrapped her in a hug, laughing. Mac ducked his head out of the kitchen and Andromeda moved to give him a big hug as well before releasing him.

"I don't think you're going to have to testify," she told him. "Mozi signed the plea agreement and turned over his family. SWAT is getting ready to serve warrants now.

Within a couple of hours, the entire terrorist cell could be no more. All those babies are finally going to get justice."

Columbus was a great city, but its greatness had been marred by the attacks. It would be epic if they could get vindication for the families.

Roz had driven through and bought Italian for dinner, which Mac was heating up in her oven. Andromeda's mouth watered at the garlic aroma. "That smells so good! I haven't eaten for hours. I'm going to go change real quick and I'll update you."

Shucking her business suit, she slipped on a pair of jeans and a red OSU sweatshirt, as well as a pair of fur lined slippers, then returned to the dining room. Roz had gotten her fettuccine with grilled chicken, just how she liked it. Mac was working on an aluminum pie pan of lasagna, and Roz had gotten penne with meatballs.

"There's a sampler plate in the fridge for Parker, whenever he gets here."

"Parker is working with SWAT right now while they serve a buttload of warrants. We got a list of about fifteen people out of Mozi al Fareq and they're going to try to serve them as close to simultaneously as possible. Two of the families will probably be together, so that might make it a little easier. But Parker is good with middle-eastern dialects, so he's going along to interpret if they need it."

"Wow," Roz breathed. "I hope he doesn't get into anything physical. I know he thinks he's Superman but he's not."

Andromeda laughed. "I'll let you tell him that when you see him."

"So, you got what you wanted?"

Andromeda nodded at Mac. "More than I ever hoped for. I don't think we'll get all of the people named in the warrants, but if we can get at least some it could be massive, because those people can be investigated. It's like ripples in a pond. We investigate whoever they're connected to, see what they've done. Mike said the FBI was going to be getting involved as well."

"Damn, girl," Roz breathed in awe. "Way to go. I'm so tickled for you. This is an incredible job you've done. I know you worked your ass off on it."

"I did," she agreed. "But I'm not going to lie. I'll be happy when it's done. I mean, so many people died for this terror group to operate and try to keep themselves hidden. I just think about all the witnesses I lost and it makes me sad and infuriates me, all at once. I'm glad they're out in the light of day now. I want them to burn."

"I think we all do," Mac agreed.

After they ate and cleaned up their dinner mess, Andromeda turned on Netflix and let Roz surf. Living on the mountain top she didn't have an actual TV to watch, so she caught up when she came to Andromeda's house. Mac charged up his tablet and perused her book shelves, then settled into a comfortable chair.

Andromeda watched her phone, waiting for a text message or a call from Parker. When it finally came she bounced in her seat.

First warrant served, 3 in custody. All safe.

A few minutes later a second message pinged her phone. *4 more in custody. Shots fired, 2 injuries. Suspects in custody.*

Feds arrived, they don't like me being here. May have to pull some strings to stay.

That made Andromeda frown. What kind of strings could he pull?

PARKER DIDN'T APPRECIATE BEING MADE to cool his heels.

As soon as the feds arrived, their translator had taken his place, but the guy wasn't catching everything. Parker listened to what the crying woman was choking out between sobs and the federal translator repeated, but they weren't the same. Just where did they get this guy?

Parker motioned to the CPD's SWAT team captain, a competent man with hard eyes. "Just to put a bug in your ear, she says there are three kids in the apartment, all under the age of six. The federally sanctioned brainiac just reported that there are six kids under the age of three. You might think about passing it on unofficial-like to your men so they're not tearing the building down looking for more kids than we've got."

Robertson snorted and shook his head. "I'll pass it on. Thanks, Quinn."

They conducted the raid on the apartment. Four adult women came out, three of them carrying a small child. The fourth woman was pregnant. But there was no one else in the apartment.

Captain Robertson immediately went to his chief, Bill Bellus. Parker saw the men talking, then Robertson motioned to Parker. The chief's face darkened, and he headed toward the Federal Agent in Charge, Nelson Tate. The gray haired man with the standard issue FBI earpiece prominently displayed and the ubiquitous FBI jacket had taken over the operation as soon as he arrived.

"Tate," Bellus snapped. "Your interpreter is feeding us bad intel. He said there were six kids in there."

Tate turned a resigned look on Chief Bellus. "They must have moved the kids out, Chief."

"Or your interpreter doesn't know what he's talking about. Our man Quinn said there were three kids under six. Look over there, Agent Tate. Do you see three kids or six?"

Tate glared at Bellus, but the Chief stood firm, heavy arms crossed, waiting expectantly.

"Three kids, Bellus. Everyone is entitled to make the occasional mistake."

"Not when it comes to the safety of my men," he growled. "I'll be using Quinn from now on."

The agent scowled. "He's not even a part of your department. You told me you just met the man tonight."

"And over the past three hours he has proven to me how valuable he is. If I need to I'll swear him into service right now."

Parker tried not to grin at the AIC, but it was hard.

After four years gone, his touch with languages was a little rusty, but it came back the more he used it. And he'd used it a lot tonight. They'd taken seven suspects into custody, as well as another six people of interest. The women they'd just rousted out of the apartment were neither, just neighbors that might have seen something, but who needed to be approached with caution.

Bellus motioned Quinn over. "Do you mind wading through this mess with us? I can either swear you in as an auxiliary officer or list you as a private contractor."

Parker thought about the two options. "I think contractor would be better for both of us."

Bellus held out his hand and they shook.

"Agent Tate has agreed to sideline his interpreter. Haven't you Agent Tate?"

"For now," the man agreed. He left their little group to talk to the kid that was supposed to be his interpreter.

The captain glanced at Parker out of the corner of his eye. "I appreciate the work you've done tonight, Quinn. You've made all of our lives easier. And safer, which is the most important thing. Once we're back on regular office hours we'll find that punk that the prosecutor's office uses. I've left him half a dozen messages at the on-call number, but he apparently turns his phone off when it's inconvenient."

"I'm not worried about it. I'll stay on the job as long as you need me."

Parker's legs throbbed, not to mention his side. The pain pill had worn off hours ago. He glanced at the clock on the wall of the command van. It was creeping toward midnight, and they still hadn't found everyone they were looking for. They hadn't found Mozi's father, for one, or Ibrahim, the brother that had helped him set up the art fair attack. Those were the two they needed the most, and no one had 'seen' them.

They had apprehended Mozi's mother and sisters. He had a feeling if he pressed the right buttons he could get them to talk. As well as the two teens that had attacked them in the park. Parker followed Bellus out of the van and toward the subjects.

CHAPTER 16

ANDROMEDA ROUSED at the first ring of her phone. "Yes."

"Hey, gorgeous. Can you talk to your doorman and approve me?"

She laughed, blinking the tiredness from her eyes. "Of course. Put him on."

There was silence for a moment.

"Ms. Pierce?"

"Hey, Hampton. That's Mr. Quinn you're speaking to and he is absolutely allowed up to my condo. Thank you so much for being cautious."

"No problem, Ms. Pierce. I'll key him up now."

Andromeda wrapped a robe over her pjs and padded to the front door. She opened it just as Parker got off the elevator.

The poor thing looked so tired, and his limp was overly pronounced. He didn't brace his hand against the wall, but it looked like he wanted to. "Oh, baby. I knew you were going to do too much."

When he reached her door, she slipped one of his arms

over her shoulders, then tilted her head up for a quick kiss. It was as natural as breathing, that kiss.

After securing the door she led him inside the condo. He looked around curiously. "Mac and Roz?"

"Roz is in the spare bedroom, and Mac is on the sofa in my office."

She glanced at the clock on the wall. Almost two a.m. "I have food in the fridge for you in you want it, or you can head straight to bed."

"Let's go lay down."

Sounded good to her. As soon as they were in the bedroom, though, and he started shucking his clothes, she realized he'd ripped open the bandage. It had brightened with fresh blood. "Why don't you go take a quick shower and I'll get Roz's medical kit from the dining room."

He saluted her.

"I'm craving a nice hot shower," he admitted. "I'll be back in a few."

Andromeda beat him back, of course, then just listened to him bathe. Years ago, they'd have showered together, and she wondered if he needed help now. Just as she thought about knocking on the door to ask, the shower shut off. Within just a couple of minutes Parker limped out.

Oh, good heavens he was something. Even a little hunched in pain, his skin gleamed in the bedroom light. He had a towel wrapped around his lean hips, holding it with one hand. The other hand held his sidearm. It was normally a good sized towel for her, but on him it looked small. And that allowed her see the too numerous torture scars, spiking her anger all over again.

"Your poor body," she sighed.

"It got a workout today," he admitted. "I didn't do anything too strenuous, but I've been on my feet and going for a long time. And it hurts trying not to limp too much, you know? I don't want them to think I can't do the job."

"You're translating. That shouldn't require anything physical. Sit down or lay down."

She motioned to the mattress and he sat on the edge, a fist wrapped in the towel around his hips. The towel was just low enough that she could reach his wound. He turned to the side a little so that she could reach both the front and the back and set his weapon on the nightstand.

Andromeda glanced at it, but it didn't cause her alarm anymore. She knew if used correctly it would save lives.

"It doesn't look like you ripped any stitches out, but it does look like you strained them, pulling on the edges of the wound." She leaned around to the back and blotted with the wipe. "Oh, looks like you pulled one here."

"Yeah, I thought I felt one give," he sighed.

"The wound looks like it held, though. We'll have Roz look at it tomorrow."

Rummaging through Roz's bag, she found two large anti-stick bandages, as well as tape. Once she had the patches in place she repacked the bag and set it aside.

"When is the last time you took anything for pain?"

He waved a hand as he shifted to a horizontal position, grimacing as he moved. "I'm going to pass on the pills. It's manageable right now."

"Bottle of water? Or anything?"

He smiled up at her, even as his body began to relax. "I'll take a bottle of water and you curling up beside me."

Andromeda hurried to get the chilled bottle of water, but by the time she returned he was deeply asleep. Smiling softly, she set the bottle on the bedside table within his reach, then circled to the other side. After debating for a moment she left her sleep pants on, then climbed into the bed beside him, wrapping her arm high over his chest.

Now that he was home she could relax and stop worrying.

PARKER BLINKED HIS EYES OPEN, his heart racing. He struggled to shake off the dream, not sure if what he'd heard was real or imagined. It was like when you were just drifting off to sleep and you imagined your mother hollering your name. *'Par-kerrrr'*. And you're jerked to consciousness.

Some instinct urged him to get up out of the bed, to do something.

There was another small click, then a rustle of fabric. Maybe Mac or Roz had gotten up to use the bathroom or get a drink of water. No, they didn't normally get up in the night. He didn't think it was either one of them.

Slipping out of the bed, he crossed to the bathroom doorway and pulled on his canvas pants, gun at the ready. Then, moving ever so slowly, he padded behind the bedroom door. Just as he got there, it began to swing open. Parker stilled and stopped breathing, waiting. The muzzle of a gun appeared first. Parker recognized a Glock, a pretty idiot proof weapon. Then a hand. But it wasn't enough. He waited as the person crept in further. Then he saw them reach to the side and flick on the lights.

Parker had half a second to recognize the surprised face of Ibrahim al Fareq, Mozi's brother, before the man began to swing his weapon toward Parker. Recognizing the immediate threat, Parker squeezed the trigger.

The HK barked in his hand, and he had a split second

of 'oh, shit, the cops needed him' before the bullet hit in the left pectoral. Parker knew immediately it was a heart shot.

Andromeda cried out as she scrambled off the bed, her eyes wild with fear as the blinked the scene into focus. Parker held up a hand, shushing her, and she clamped a hand over her mouth. Nodding, her eyes burning with fury and fear, she backed against the wall of glass.

Now that he knew she was out of the immediate danger, Parker leaned out enough to look down the hallway. He could see there were shadows moving, but he couldn't tell what was going on.

Then he heard several hard thumps from next door, and fear lanced through him. He glanced at Andromeda and could see she realized what was happening as well. Roz was in the next room.

"You should come out now, Army man," a voice called down the hallway, "before anyone else gets hurt."

Parker clenched his jaw, not liking the direction this was going. He peered down the hallway again, and grimaced. Roz was dancing on tiptoes as the man behind her, several inches taller and many pounds stronger, gripped her head in his arm. His left hand was clamped over her mouth and his weapon was pressed against her right temple.

Tears leaked from her terrified eyes and Parker swore. She didn't deserve this.

"What do you want, al Fareq?"

"Ah, of course you know who I am. That is good. It will make things go more smoothly. Step out here, Army man."

Parker took a step forward, fury surging in him, gun at his side. If he was lucky the other man wouldn't see it. Why did he keep calling him an Army man?

"And where is Prosecutor Pierce? I know she's here. Invite her out."

Parker glanced at Andromeda, who moved up. She bent down to the intruder's body for a second, then stood again. The man was long dead, but his maybe father didn't need to know that.

"Your son is bleeding," Parker told him, "and you're holding the only medical personnel capable of saving him. Why don't you let her go?"

There was a long stretch of silence.

"Ah, well, Ibrahim is just going to have to give his life for the cause, because this woman," he paused to run the gun muzzle through her hair, "is staying exactly where she is. Now, where is Prosecutor Pierce? Where is the woman responsible for all of the turmoil of this night?"

Parker could feel her moving up beside him. She paused to look at him for a second, before peering around the doorjamb.

"Ah, there she is. Step forward, please. Take the Army man's weapon from his right hand, first."

Parker could have cursed a blue streak, but he handed Andromeda the gun. Her fingers barely wrapped around the grip. Shaking, she held the weapon in one hand. "Please let her go," she said, her voice raspy from sleep and maybe from the scream.

"I don't think I can do that," the older man said, and he almost sounded like he was laughing.

Now that his eyes had adjusted to the light, he could see that the man had to be in his fifties, at least. His hair had grayed out, and he wore a long gray beard. His dark eyes were cold, and Parker could see an endless number of deaths in their depths. This man had done every heinous thing imaginable and was willing to do more.

"You have cost me the lives of my family. My children, my wife, they are all in custody now because of you."

Andromeda shook her head. "No, because of Mozi, your son. He told us where they all were."

The old man clenched his teeth. "*Harum zadeh*. He is no son of mine. Do not even mention his name to me again. Step forward."

Al Fareq pressed the muzzle into Roz's temple harder, making her whimper.

Andromeda held up a hand in supplication and took a small step forward, then stopped.

That seemed to satisfy al Fareq because he gave her a grimy smile. "Now, I'm going to give you a chance to get out of this."

Parker felt his fear spike for Andromeda. He knew she would do anything to get Roz out of this, even at the expense of her own safety. He glanced at her narrow back, almost directly in front of him.

"You have one chance to lift that gun and take a shot at me," al Fareq told her. "Assuming, of course, you don't shoot your friend in the process."

The old man chuckled. Parker knew Andromeda's face had to be fearful, but she shook her head.

"I'm not going to do that you fucking asshole." Her voice had taken on a thread of steel. "Instead, I'm going to give you one chance to surrender your weapon and let the woman go."

Parker's heart began to race and he reached out toward Andromeda. He had to be ready for anything.

The old man barked out a laugh. "I admire your courage, Prosecutor Pierce, but I decline your offer. Now what are you going to do?"

"Nothing," she said softly. Then she tossed Parker's gun toward al Fareq's feet.

Everything slowed down to microseconds. The old

man's eyes followed the path of the gun as it arced toward his feet. As soon as it hit the floor the gun went off, because Parker had lightened the trigger pull. The apartment echoed with the sound of the gunshot, which had struck off in the dark somewhere. Parker reached out and grabbed the Glock from the back waistband of Andromeda's sleep pants, even as she dove to the side to get out of the line of fire. As Parker raised the dead man's weapon, Roz's fist shot out and down, hitting the old man in the crotch almost perfectly, but the more devastating strike came from Mac. The former Army Ranger's ham sized fist struck the old man's temple from behind, knocking him out cold. He hadn't even seen him coming.

Parker jerked the gun up and away without firing a shot.

Roz staggered but Mac was there to catch her, wrapping her into his massive arms. She sagged into him instantly.

Parker dropped the gun and went to Andromeda. She sat up, tears streaking down her face as she realized it was over. She staggered to her feet and lunged at Roz, hugging her from behind. The two women turned to each other, and Parker held his fist out to Mac. Knocking bruised knuckles, the man grinned at him.

"That felt good," he rumbled.

CHAPTER 17

To SAY that her apartment was in an uproar would be an understatement. Suddenly she was smack in the middle of a crime scene.

The police department arrived first, because they were already on scene, technically; they just hadn't been in exactly the right places. While they'd been in the parking garage and at the secondary exit doors, the terrorists had walked into the front door and simply overwhelmed the guard, stealing his master key card. Hampton would probably be fine, but he was on his way to the hospital with a severe concussion.

Ali al Fareq lay quietly on the floor, still unconscious from Mac's fist to his head. Parker had tied his hands behind his back with an electrical cord after he'd checked him for weapons, but he hadn't so much as twitched yet. Andromeda doubted that he would for a while. Paramedics were checking him over and Parker's impromptu restraint was being replaced by actual handcuffs, thanks to a Columbus PD officer. The officer looked dazed, like he didn't even know where to begin.

Andromeda glanced at her phone. Creeping toward four a.m. It had been forty minutes since everything had gone down, and she was still shaking. Mike was on his way, as was the FBI. She'd sent him a recording of the entire incident. Actually, when she'd been so sharply woken, it was like the adrenaline had kicked her brain into gear as fast as possible. Not even thinking about it, she'd grabbed her phone and keyed up the camera to video. You couldn't see anything through the fabric of her sleep pants, but the conversation came through crisp and clear.

The four of them sat on the barstools at the kitchen peninsula. Parker held her hand in a death grip, and she allowed him. She needed that connection right now.

Roz sat on her other side holding Mac's hand, though she still wiped away tears occasionally. After being attacked before, Andromeda had a feeling it would take her a while to get over this incident.

Andromeda needed to do something, rather than stare at the paramedics checking al Fareq over. "I'm going to make coffee," she said abruptly, sliding off the stool.

The cop looked at her in alarm, but Andromeda waved him away. "We need coffee," she grumbled, "and the kitchen is not part of the crime scene."

Okay, *technically* it probably was, but she needed coffee. They could growl at her later.

She started running cups under the single serve Keurig and changing pods. She had an actual pot somewhere, but she couldn't even begin to remember where she'd put it. She never used it.

She sugared and creamed Roz's cup. Left Mac's black, just the way he liked it, and gave Parker a black with sugar. Then she made up her own, with an extra heavy splash of cream. And she returned to her stool, where they waited for people in charge.

The police officer's sergeant arrived first, then the Chief of Police. The big man went to Parker first, shaking his hand.

"Tell me what's going on."

Andromeda thought it was telling that he went to Parker before even one of his own officers. He knew to get his information from the horse's mouth.

Parker recapped everything and asked for Andromeda to play the audio. After she swiped the phone off, the chief shook his head at her. "That was smart thinking."

She sighed and nodded. "I knew it would need to be airtight if any of this went to court."

"I don't know many women that would have thought that far ahead in the situation you were in."

Andromeda laughed. "I'm a prosecuting attorney. Of course I did."

Mike arrived shortly after that, then a whole slew of crime techs and photographers. She wanted, needed, clothes, but they wouldn't let her into her bedroom. It was a crime scene. Instead she went into the entryway closet and dug through spare clothes she had stored there. She found a pair of jeans that were a little tight, a bra in a plastic bag that hadn't made it to Salvation Army yet, and a gray sweatshirt from the same bag. She was pretty much set.

When she returned to the living room, there were even more people in her house. She wove through them to get to Parker, and he gripped her hand.

He was a port in a storm, standing so strong against everything going on. She climbed up onto the stool and waited to be interviewed.

CHAPTER 18

PARKER LOST track how many people asked him the same questions over and over again, but he understood the reasoning. They had to get everything exactly right. If they let even one terrorist or unexplored connection fall through their fingers it could mean more deaths, and no one wanted that.

Ali al Fareq was transported to the hospital, and his son Ibrahim was carted off by the coroner. Parker's weapon was logged into evidence, after they allowed him to make the weapon safe. He sighed as he watched the tech carry it away. Hopefully he would get it back soon. He really liked that gun.

Andromeda disappeared for a few minutes and when she returned she had changed clothes. She looked warmer and more secure in herself, and she didn't sag once as she repeated the same details he had about what had happened. Andromeda stood with Roz as she was interviewed, holding her hand tightly. When the detective interviewing her asked Andromeda to step away she told him he could go suck a dick, because it wasn't happening. She wasn't leaving her best friend.

Mac's story was the only one that changed. It wasn't until the coroner was leaving that Mac mentioned the other body in the office. The responding cop turned red because he hadn't known about the third assailant, and it made him look like a putz. Mac had shrugged when asked and explained that after he'd struck the man's gun hand away, he slammed a fist into the man's chest. He explained rather clinically that it had apparently stopped the man's heart. He'd read about the technique but had never actually tried it himself.

Parker snorted. Mac actually sounded impressed that it had worked. He was very thankful for the man's big hands tonight.

Okay, that sounded weird.

Mac now sat on the couch, holding Roz against his side. He seemed to be willing to do anything for her, and it made Parker's heart happy.

Andromeda was talking something over with Mike, their heads bent over her computer, which had thankfully been out here. The chief had pulled some strings and let the techs give him his cellphone.

"There's nothing you need it for," the man had growled when one of them had argued.

It rang in his pocket now, and Parker knew who it would be before he even looked at the screen.

"Yes, Commander."

Lambert chuckled on the other end of the line. "How did you know it was me? You didn't even look at it."

Damn this guy was spooky. Parker glanced out the lightening wall of windows looking out over the Scioto River. "You always call me at the worst times."

Lambert chuckled. "Why is it the worst time? You're one of the heroes of the hour. I saw some of the crime scene photos. That was a hell of a shot. Right through the heart. There was no saving him. And the punch that Ranger gave the old man actually left divots in his skull. They're not sure if al Fareq is going to make it or not."

"Hm," Parker responded. "No loss if he doesn't."

"Well, I hope he does. We have a place we can take a man like him to get answers." He paused. "You did a good job, Parker. Better than I expected."

Parker snorted. "Gee, thanks for the compliment."

"I mean it. You took out a huge cell of terrorists. ISIS will feel this. It's one less foothold they have in America."

"Yes," Parker sighed, "I suppose you're right."

Suddenly he felt tired. Bone deep weary. And there was no end to this mess in sight. They needed to come up with a place to stay tonight for the four of them. And they needed clothing and all the other little stupid stuff they couldn't get to.

"Is that all you needed, Lambert? I'm pretty tired. Gonna get my girl and find us a place to chill for a few days."

"Already done. That's why I called. I rented you a couple of rooms at the Westin Columbus, just a few blocks away. Presidential suite and a junior suite right next door. They're awaiting your arrival. There's even a car downstairs to take you all there. I assume Ms. White and Mr. Mackenzie will be going with you."

Rather than fight the inevitable, Parker decided to accept the gift graciously. "I appreciate that, Lambert. That's very human of you."

Lambert chuckled. "Enjoy yourself, Parker. You've earned it. I'll be in touch."

Parker was sure he would.

Andromeda seemed relieved to have a place to go, but she didn't want to take the car provided. She wanted to take her own Range Rover. Parker didn't blame her. Her apartment would be off limits indefinitely and it was hard to tell when they would allow her to get anything from it.

Mike went down in the elevator with them as they left. There was a police officer in the monitor on the elevator.

"I need to check on Hampton," Andromeda murmured.

"I'm sure he's fine."

She didn't seem convinced. She and Parker got into the Range Rover, and Mac took the keys from Roz for her vehicle.

"It's just at the Westin, Mac," Andromeda told him. "Directly east."

He saluted and helped Roz up into her truck. The woman still seemed dazed, but she would rally.

When Parker went to the front desk of the Westin, they were greeted like rock stars and shown upstairs almost immediately. Mac escorted Roz into the suite beside theirs. "Let's chill out for a couple of hours and meet for a late breakfast."

"Sounds good," Parker told him.

Lambert hadn't been lying when he'd said they'd taken care of everything. Inside the suite there were clothes and toiletries, snacks and beverages, alcohol, everything imaginable for a traveler in need. Andromeda looked at the stuff scattered around and shook her head. "How?"

"My former boss," Parker said simply. "He's trying to make our life easier."

"That's awful nice of him," she murmured. "Your former SEAL boss?"

Parker sighed. "Well, kinda. He's actually working for the CIA right now."

Her dark brows shot into her hairline. "CIA?"

Parker nodded grimly, and Andromeda laughed.

"Did the FBI know you were working for the CIA?"

Parker chuckled with her. "Hell, no."

"Hm."

Crossing the room, she dropped down onto the long, overstuffed gray couch, then dragged a blanket down over top of her. Parker sat down beside her and she rested her head on his shoulder. "I'm emotionally wrought," she murmured. "I want all this to go away but I know it's not going to."

He stroked his hand through her hair. "You've done an excellent job, with everything. I meant to tell you that earlier. The gun in your back waistband was inspired. If Mac hadn't have intervened I would have had to, and it may not have turned out as well. I'm a good shot, but that would have been difficult. It's been a while since I was in a situation like that."

"You did just as well. I had no idea what to do but you kept everything controlled. And you saved my life." She pulled back to look at him. "I never thanked you for that."

Parker pulled her to him, pressing a kiss to upturned mouth. "I had to save you. We have a lot of unfinished business."

A slow smile spread across her lips, then a shadow slid across her expression. "I kind of don't want it all to end."

He pulled back in surprise. "What?"

She heaved a breath.

"I don't want you to leave," she admitted finally.

Parker's throat tightened, and it was all he could do to

swallow. "I know what you mean," he whispered. "I want us to make do with what we have now. I'm not leaving tomorrow. I'll stay at least a week, even if I have to take vacation from my other job. It may take that long for a lot of things to happen. We'll know more about al Fareq's condition, all of the warrants will have been served by then, hopefully. I have a feeling I have a lot more work to do before I can get out of here."

She nodded, giving him a playful smile. "Then I suggest we take advantage of it. I've been looking at your half naked body all week and I haven't been able to do anything about it. Can we make something beautiful come out of this morning?"

Damn, she really knew where to hit Parker where it hurt. Right in the heart. "I think that's a wonderful idea, but..."

"No buts, damn it. I've been waiting patiently while you recovered, and then you were tired, and then we had to kill people. We're as secure as we're going to get, aren't we? And I'm too amped up to do anything else."

Parker laughed as she shivered, but the smile abruptly faded from his face as she went to her knees before him. She braced her arms over his thighs as she began to push the t-shirt up his abs. Parker shifted and tugged the shirt over his head, tossing it away. His side hurt, but less than it did the day before. He was getting stronger with every hour and he wanted to be everything he could be for her.

"I have to warn you," he said eventually as her fingers stroked down his center line. "I'm not as pretty as I used to be."

Andromeda grinned up at him. "Pretty, huh? You weren't handsome?"

"I was both of those things, but that was before Yemen.

I'm serious, Andromeda. He fucked me up everywhere, not just where you can see."

For a moment her eyes hardened with anger, then she smiled at him. "It won't bother me, Parker. I'm just glad you're here. You have to know that."

"Yeah," he sighed. "I know."

And honestly, he was glad he was here too, even though he was feeling very exposed. Even as the thought registered, he reached for the remote on the table beside him and closed the blinds, sealing off the view of the city. Andromeda would probably think it was because of his scars, but it was more because of Lambert. It was hard to tell what the man would spy on if he thought it would serve a purpose.

Andromeda sat back on her heels to untie his boots. She tugged them off and tossed them away, then moved up to the zipper of his BDUs. Before he could delay her any more she had unzipped his pants and was working to pull them down his legs.

Parker lifted his butt to help her out, then watched as she tossed those away as well. He hadn't time to pull on underwear in the midst of the attack, so he was bare to her and the world. Before he could cover himself with a hand, she'd parked herself in the same pose as before, arms over his thighs and her leaning between them. Her eyes rested on the mass of scars on his lower belly, then down his length.

"Even here?" she whispered.

Parker sighed as she stroked a finger over the faint tracing of white lines down the most sensitive part of him. "Yes. Those healed well, though." He rested a hand on his lower belly. "These took longer because they got infected."

She cupped Parker's hard length in her hand and leaned

forward to press kisses along the length, smiling slightly as he hardened even more in her hand.

"He's still happy to see me," she murmured.

"Of course, he's happy to see you. Plus, well... it's been a long time."

Her golden eyes looked up at him, considering. "How long has it been?"

Parker made a face. "Well, I hadn't been with anyone for a while before Yemen, so it's been at least five years."

He shivered as she pressed her lips to the thick vein running up the underside. "Oh, babe. No wonder why you are so hard."

Parker let his head fall back against the couch cushion as she explored him. He knew he wasn't as visually pleasing as before, and it worried him. Andromeda was a beautiful woman and she deserved to have someone at her side equally as beautiful, but there was no way he was going to give up this time with her. He would fight through his embarrassment and give her all of the pleasure he possibly could before he had to leave.

She did something with her mouth and he jerked, pleasure roaring through him. His side twinged but it was a distant pain. This wasn't fair to her but fuck, it felt good. He would indulge just for a minute.

Parker squeezed his legs around her and reached down to cup her head in his hands. She looked up at him, her brilliant eyes shining in pleasure. Looking down the line of her body he knew she was aroused. Her hips shifted suggestively, as if she wanted to touch herself.

Gripping her arms, Parker pulled her up toward him. Andromeda made a sad sound as he pulled her away from his hardness, but he didn't allow her to sway him. "Take off your clothes."

Her eyes glowing with excitement, she stood before him and began to undress. She should have looked ridiculous pulling the sweatshirt over her head, but he focused on her breasts. Andromeda had always been long and lean, but she'd had the prettiest little natural breasts. He was very glad she didn't appear to have changed that. As she peeled every layer over her head, her breasts became more visible, until he was holding his breath as she pulled the plain beige bra away from her chest. Oh, yes, there they were. Perfectly proportioned, perfectly shaped, just enough to fill his hand. Parker wanted her to move closer, but she wouldn't until she'd taken everything off.

The pants were tight, but they reminded him of being a kid in junior high and seeing all the girls in their skintight stonewashed jeans walking down the hallways. He'd had an appreciation for the female shape ever since then. Andromeda's gently rounded hips aroused him like no other.

She knew it, too. Slowly, seductively, she bent over as she pushed the jeans down over her hips then down the length of her legs. Her lace panties followed the same path, then got tossed with his own clothes somewhere across the room.

For a moment she stood before him perfectly exposed, her body drawing him in like it always did. Parker's dick bounced, needing her. Her eyes flicked down and that smile spread across her lips. Her eyes damn near luminous, she moved toward him.

Parker shifted down on the couch and held a hand out to her. "Straddle me."

She grinned as she went to one knee beside him, lifted the other over his lap and reached down to angle him into her. Parker knew he was walking on the edge and there was a very real chance he would explode as soon as he felt her hot, wet heat around him, but he wanted her this way the first time. It had been so long since he'd seen her body. He just wanted to look at her for a while.

Andromeda began to lower herself onto him, but she stilled just as he breached her outer labia. Parker groaned, his hands going to her hips, but she held firm above him. Bracing a hand on his chest, she looked him in the eye. "I've missed you, Parker."

Then, with a gentle bounce, she began working him inside herself. Parker gritted his teeth, fighting off his orgasm. Then she slid all the way down his length and they both groaned. Sinuously, seductively, Andromeda began to move her body. Parker tweaked her nipples, making her gasp and tighten around him. Wrapping his hands down over her ass cheeks, he started dragging her forward on the down stroke. Andromeda cried out and started moving more aggressively, riding him hard. Again, Parker knew there would be pain later, but he couldn't help but move beneath her, shoving himself as deep as he could.

Andromeda began to pant and jerk, then she cupped her own breasts and arched back. Parker reached for the dark cloud of hair that blended into his and stroked. Her clit was so swollen and hungry for attention. Angling his hand to fit against her, he probed with a finger. He felt his own hardness, as well as the silken glide of her body. Then he flicked her clit with his fingertip.

It was almost like she'd been waiting for that single touch. Gasping, Andromeda cried out, her body straining in his lap. Parker held onto her as the orgasm caused her skin to shudder and ripple with gooseflesh. Internally, her sheath clutched at his cock and he couldn't keep his orgasm back in the face of her pleasure. Groaning, Parker emptied himself into her, hands clutching at her hips spasmodically.

Andromeda rolled her head to look at him and braced her arms against his shoulders, her eyes heavy-lidded. "As always, you were amazing, but you make me want more."

She leaned down and kissed him on the lips, her fingers running over his jaw. Parker blinked up at her, loving the look on her face. "Well, let me recover from this one first," he laughed.

Andromeda slipped off of his lap and the aches began to settle in, but he wasn't going to let it tarnish the experience. Sitting up, he took her offered hand. "Let's go take a shower."

CHAPTER 19

Mac DIDN'T KNOW what to do about Roz. She seemed...
brittle, and he worried that if he did anything she would
completely shatter. He held her hand as he led her into the
suite. There were supplies stocked on one of the counters.
Looked like clothing and food and toiletries. A little bit of
everything. There were even a couple of books, it looked
like. He glanced at her, wondering if he dared let go of her
hand. She'd had a death grip on it for the past two hours.

"Don't give me that look," she complained.

Mac paused in surprise. "What look?"

"Like you're going to have to Google the closest looney
bin. I'm okay, just shook up."

Deliberately, she opened her hand and moved away,
checking the rooms. Then she went into the bathroom and
he heard water running.

Mac felt for her. He really did. She'd been attacked
before, he was pretty sure, and this would just bring all that
trauma back up. He knew she'd had some kind of settlement
with her former work, but not what the details were. He
wished he did. Maybe he could help her better.

Crossing to the concierge counter, he powered up the little single serve Keurig. Maybe an herbal tea, right now. No coffee.

When Roz exited the bathroom, her face had been washed and she looked a little more clear-eyed. Mac handed her the insulated cup. "Sugar? Or milk? It's herbal tea."

She blinked down at the cup. "Maybe some sugar."

He handed her a couple of packets, then waved her to the couch. She sank down into it and set the tea aside. Mac could see how tired she was, so he hoped that if she got warm and relaxed she would fall back asleep. It had been a late night, and an even earlier morning for them. They needed more rest.

Making a cup of tea for himself, he doctored it up, then sank into the armchair at the end of the couch. Cradling the cup in his hands he let his head fall back against the cushions.

It had been crazy in Andromeda's apartment for a while. When he'd heard the snick of the door mechanism and seen the shadow moving into his room, he'd reacted on pure instinct. As soon as he'd recognized the threat he'd done what he'd needed to in order to take it out. Him out. Mac didn't know if he was supposed to feel bad or not. He definitely did not. The lives of three friends and countless other innocents were still here because he'd done what he'd done.

Then when he'd crept out and seen the gray-haired man holding Roz at gunpoint, he'd been livid. She didn't even like men in her house. He couldn't imagine how she was feeling with a man she didn't know about to kill her, his arms holding her captive.

"I haven't thanked you for what you did," she murmured suddenly.

Ah, they were both thinking about the incident. He rolled his head up and looked at her.

"I didn't do anything. I think between what you did and what Parker was about to do, everything would have turned out okay without my intervention."

Roz looked at him directly. "Parker would have taken a shot that may or may not have struck me, you and I both know it. He would have done anything to protect Andromeda."

Mac looked at her, frowning. "I think you underestimate Parker. He would have hit him. I don't think he wanted to, though, because that would have been the end of the investigation. It's hard to question a dead man."

Like the guy on Andromeda's office floor.

"I think," he continued, "everything happened the way it needed to. Perfectly. You hitting him the way you did gave everyone else a direction to follow. I'm very proud of you for doing that."

Suddenly her eyes filled with tears and she nodded. "I can't tell you how scared I was. But I couldn't let it just happen again."

Rocking forward in his chair, Mac held a hand out to her. He wasn't sure if she would take it or not, but he would offer her every bit of comfort she would take.

Roz blinked and stared at his hand. Mac could see the internal struggle, but she reached out anyway. She'd been holding his hand for hours after the incident, but when she'd gained a little perspective and distance she'd started to close up and retreat back into herself. He didn't want that. He curled his fingers around her own.

Then she surprised him by tugging on his hand. Following her pull, Mac left the chair and sat on the couch beside her. Then, totally disarming him, she curled in against his chest.

Mac's heart was pounding because less than four hours ago he had killed a man, but she was turning to him for comfort. As his arms settled around her oh, so gently, he decided they both needed the comfort. For a long time they just sat there, sharing warmth and support. Mac didn't think she was crying, but she was definitely trembling, and he was very careful not to do any more than what she'd given him.

"I want to go back to my cabin, Mac," she whispered. "I *need* to go back to my cabin."

His heart sank at the thought of her leaving. "I understand. Completely. If I had that option I would as well. There's a very strong healing energy there."

She was silent for a long time. "Y-you're welcome to come back with me."

Mac thought he had misheard. "I'm sorry?"

"You're welcome to come back with me," she said more strongly. "I think I might like the company. Andromeda will be staying with Parker, but I can't stay here." She drew back to look him in the eyes. "Will you go back to the cabin with me for a while?"

How could he deny her anything? Her big blue eyes were laden with heartbreak, and a strong dash of fear. Without even stopping to consider what he was agreeing to, he nodded his head. "Of course I will. Besides," he paused. "You still haven't given me the recipe for your biscuits."

That startled a laugh from her and a squeeze around the neck, then she pulled away.

"I'm going to go lay down for a while."

A flicker of fear crossed her face and Mac knew what it

was. He'd seen that look on men he'd served with. "If you leave your door open, I'll be right here reading my book."

Relief eased through her expression and she nodded. Walking into the bedroom she pushed the door almost shut. Mac could see the bed coverings moving as she climbed into the bed and covered up. He sighed as he pulled a book from his pocket and debated getting coffee to stay awake for her.

Who needed sleep anyway?

CHAPTER 20

IT WAS AMAZINGLY easy to settle back into a relationship with Parker and that scared the shit out of Andromeda, because in a day or three, whenever he finished his work for the police department, he would be leaving.

It had been a week since everything had gone down. They'd released her apartment to her two days ago, and the cleaning crew had gotten done with it yesterday. As she walked through the rooms now, she thought she'd be skeeved out or something that a guy had been killed in her bedroom but being a pragmatic woman, she really wasn't. He'd been trying to kill her, so she was glad that he'd died and she hadn't. And it wasn't like she'd known him. She hadn't even seen the one in her office, so it was easy to put that one out of her mind as well.

The same with the living room hallway, where al Fareq had held Roz hostage. There were no signs of the incident at all, and since Roz was okay, it didn't really feel like a crime scene.

If that made sense. She wasn't even sure anymore.

Roz had gone back to West Virginia. Even though

they'd been in a hotel, she'd had to get away from the city, she said. Andromeda could understand. A lot of traumatic things had happened to her here. The surprising thing was, Mac went back with her. They weren't dating or anything— she didn't even think they'd kissed— but they liked each other's company. Mac didn't have anything holding him here anymore, with the trial cancelled. The cops were done interviewing the two of them and no charges would be filed against Zane Mackenzie in the death of the as yet unnamed assailant.

Andromeda understood that Mac could be Roz's security for now, and she didn't want either one of them subjected to the news and hubbub here.

Her own job, no, her *professional image*, had undergone a huge shift. Andromeda had been known around the office as a workaholic and even a little cold, but after the incident in her apartment and all the raids that had changed. Janie, her assistant, had come into the office one day last week and she'd been literally bouncing with excitement.

"I wanted to catch you up on the gossip," she said, settling into the chair in front of Andromeda's desk and crossing her legs.

"Okay, what is it?"

Andromeda rocked back in her chair and crossed her arms. Janie had done this before and it usually pertained to a man that she'd shut down calling her frigid or a tease.

"You now have *street cred*," Janie whispered, leaning forward.

"What?"

Janie widened her eyes dramatically. "Your reputation has climbed significantly, especially with the women in the building. Between the Navy SEAL warming your bed and escorting you everywhere, and you taking down a huge terrorist cell in the city, as well as killing a dude in your condo, you should be getting your People's Choice Award literally any minute."

Andromeda laughed because it was so preposterous, shaking her head as she rocked forward in her chair. "I didn't kill anyone..."

Janie waved that off. "Near enough. You helped. I have to thank you because it wasn't always easy in this job but even *my* reputation has undergone a shift as well. The rest of the office staff is hoping I catch you in a sexy clinch with your man."

Andromeda laughed again and nodded her head. "I'll pass that along to Parker, but you need to know he's not staying."

Janie frowned at her, her blue eyes alarmed. "Wait, what?"

She took a breath. "Parker still has his job in Denver. He's just out here helping right now."

Janie looked like she was going to cry. "But you guys love each other! It's so obvious. Why would he leave?"

Andromeda shrugged, her own throat tightening with tears. "It just never quite works out for us."

That conversation haunted her. Throughout the day she thought about what they could do differently. Parker had told her several times how much he loved working with the group in Denver. After hearing about him talk about them so much she felt like she knew all of the people that worked there. They had given him hope for a future at a time when he desperately needed it.

He would never leave them.

And her job was just ramping up, seriously. Mike had several years before he could retire, but if she kept putting the criminals away like she had been there was a very strong chance she could move up. And she loved her job.

Yes, she could probably get a new job in Colorado if he asked, but Parker hadn't even asked. He hadn't even told her he loved her.

In all fairness, she hadn't told him either. It was like she was pretending that she didn't love him, just to salvage a tiny bit of her heart. They made love at least every night, but they didn't say the words. Everything but.

She glanced into the living room. They'd finished up their room service dinner from the restaurant downstairs, and she'd just called for the waiter to come get their dishes. They were sitting outside on the cart, along with the tip.

Parker had seemed distracted today and she was afraid to ask him why, because she didn't want her fears confirmed. Mozi and Ali al Fareq, as well as those rounded up on the raid, had been transported out of the state. No one was sure where, just that they had orders from way the hell high up that they were supposed to follow. Andromeda didn't care. She'd closed the Christmas Parade case and the Art Fair case, and the families had some degree of closure. Privately, Andromeda hoped that wherever they took the al Fareqs it involved pain.

She grabbed the bottle of wine they'd been working on and carried it into the living room. Parker had the TV on, but he was staring blankly at the screen, not even really seeing anything. It wasn't until she bumped him that he looked at her. "Hey, babe. Sorry. Thinking about things."

"I could tell," she murmured, refilling their glasses. "We're losing time, aren't we?"

He looked up at her, his hard, gunmetal gray eyes softening as they looked at her. "Yeah," he confirmed. "Now that the group has been shipped out my workload has diminished. I have a final interview to translate, then I'll be done."

She nodded, hating to have her fears confirmed.

"And Duncan texted me today wondering when I would be back." He took a heavy breath. "I told him the day after tomorrow."

The bottom fell out of her stomach. Setting her glass down, she cuddled in next to him. His big arms looped around her, holding her tight. "I'm not ready for you to go," she murmured.

Sighing, he pressed a kiss to the top of her head. "I know, babe. I'm not either. Let's make it a different kind of parting this time, though. No angst or blaming. We both knew this was coming. And we each made the most of it, I think. I love you, Andromeda."

Joy burst inside her heart, almost drowning out the sadness. "I love you, too," she whispered, tears seeping from her eyes. "Dammit Parker, why can't we get this right?"

"I don't know."

His voice had deepened, like he was fighting emotion as well. "And let's think about not completely ending it, okay? I mean, flights to Denver are not that expensive. There's nothing to say we can't have a long distance relationship, you know?"

It wasn't ideal, but he was right. There was no one around here vying for her attention. She nodded slowly. "Not ideal, but better than nothing. We can at least try it for a few months and see how it goes."

In bed that night Parker seemed determined to imprint upon her how perfect they were together. He kissed every square inch of her body, brought her to orgasm several times with his lips and fingers, before finally gliding into her to send her spiraling away again. Andromeda cried at the perfection of the moment. For a long time, they just held each other, waiting for sleep, but it didn't come for a long time.

———

PARKER HATED WALKING AWAY. It reminded him of last time he left, just not as much yelling. Now there was crying, but it was very different.

The bag he'd brought with him was packed and he was dressed. A car would be arriving within a few minutes to take him to the airport.

Andromeda stood before him looking strong and beautiful, as always. Hair curled over her forehead and she pushed it to the side, then crossed her arms beneath her breasts. There were tears in her golden eyes, and he hated to see them there.

"Andy, this is not a forever goodbye. You know that. I want this to be a temporary parting."

One side of her mouth tipped up in a sad smile as he cupped her face.

"Hey," he said suddenly, flicking his phone on. "I want a picture of us together. As hokey as it is, we're going to do a selfie. We've never done one before."

She sputtered, then laughed as he tried to position his phone down the length of his arm. Curling himself around her, he hit the shutter button several times, but it didn't seem to work. She turned her face into his neck, kissing him there, and wrapped her arms around him. Parker put his phone away and just held her.

The front desk guard rang the condo and they moved apart as Parker answered the phone.

"Your car is here, sir."

"Okay, thank you Hampton."

When he looked at Andy, there was resignation in her eyes. "I'll go down with you."

They held hands on the elevator. She had beautiful hands, Parker decided. Her fingers long and delicate. But strong enough to do anything that needed to be done. He thought about the past two weeks. She'd saved his life a couple of times. Gave him more pleasure than he ever could have imagined. Accepted him and his beat up old body more than he thought any woman ever could.

It made his heart ache to leave her behind.

She kissed him several times, then gave him a bone cracking hug. "Call me when you get there to let me know you made it okay."

"I will," he promised. Holding his forehead to hers, he kissed the tip of her nose. "I love you, Andromeda Pierce."

"I love you too, Parker Quinn."

Parker drew away, then, because her sadness was breaking his heart. With a final wave, he walked through the glass doors to the taxi waiting in the valet loop. When he looked back, she was gone.

DUNCAN WILDE ROCKED BACK in his office chair when Parker walked in.

"Well, lookie here. I didn't think you were coming back, Quinn."

Parker made a face. "To tell the truth, I didn't know if I was either."

He'd been back for a week now, and it just didn't feel right yet.

Duncan nodded once and leaned forward to slide some papers around on his desk, pulling a couple from the top of the stack. "I've been following what was going on out in Columbus. That is where you went, correct?"

"Yes, sir."

"Not sure why you needed to take time off to do this. The company would have covered you for the interpreting."

Parker sank down into the chair in front of Duncan's broad desk. "It was as much personal as professional. And I didn't know what I was going to be doing when I got there."

"Ah," Duncan said softly, his dark eyes considering. "I

see. Well, it looks like you did some good out there. Too good, actually."

Parker frowned. "Sir?"

"Well, I just had an interesting call from a Chief Bellus at Columbus PD, wanting to know what I paid you."

Parker knew he looked confused, but he just wasn't following.

"Because whatever it was it wasn't enough, he said. Said you did as much to put that terror cell to bed as anyone. Then he sent me a copy of a police report he thought I might be interested in."

Duncan showed him the report and from the picture at the top he could tell it was the incident in Andy's condo. "That's some damn fine cowboy work you did, Parker. I'm impressed."

Duncan smiled, and Parker had to smile with him. "Things turned out better than I expected."

"And this Andromeda Pierce sounds like a badass."

Parker thought of Andy sticking Ibrahim's gun in her waist band. "She is, sir. She really is."

Tilting his head, Duncan gave him a narrow-eyed look. "Is she important to you?"

"More important to me than breathing," he agreed immediately.

That seemed to take Duncan aback. "Really? Damn. No wonder why you dragged your feet coming back."

Duncan stood up from his chair and moved to the plate glass windows looking out over the industrial district of Denver. "Bellus told me I better be giving you a raise because he planned to hire you away from me." Duncan looked at him to gauge his reaction, but Parker didn't know what to say. "I told him he could sign a contract with Lost and Found and I would dispatch you out there as a contractor, if you were interested. Or maybe we'll just start a branch out there. Have you ever run a business, Parker?"

He frowned, his jaw going slack for a moment. "No, sir. That doesn't mean I couldn't, though," he said quickly.

Duncan grinned at him, nodding his head. "Yeah, that's what I thought you'd say."

Moving back to his desk Duncan sat down in his chair. "Talk to Shannon and set up a meeting a little later in the week. I'll talk to the other partners and feel them out about things. No promises, but we'll see what we can do to get you back there. You're too valuable for me to give you up completely, so I'm willing to work with you. Sound good?"

Parker nodded, standing to shake his hand. "Yes, sir it does. Thank you."

He walked out of the office dazed, but in a good way. His immediate thought was to call Andy, but he didn't want to get her hopes up. He would wait until after the meeting.

ANDROMEDA PACED, her heels clicking on the floor of Columbus's John Glenn Airport terminal. Parker was flying in, but his plane had been delayed and she'd been waiting for an hour.

It was her own fault, though. Parker had planned to take a car to her condo and just meet her there after she got off from work, but Andromeda thought it would be a nice surprise to meet him at the airport. She hadn't seen him for a month and a half, and she was anxious, damn it.

She glanced at the arrivals board and saw that his flight was now on the ground.

It still took a half hour to see him.

The limp was tempered by excitement, she could tell

that. He was moving more fluidly than she'd ever seen him. As she crossed the terminal to him, she waited for him to look up and see her. It only took a few seconds for him to zero in on her and when he did, his hard, off-balance face softened with love. She knew that look. She had seen it from him many times. But this time was completely different.

Parker cupped her face as soon as she was close enough, giving her a hello kiss that made people around them snicker. One younger teen told them to get a room and move out of the way.

Laughing, they moved aside, then continued reacquainting themselves. He looked at her with a frown.

"I thought I was going to your condo and meeting you there."

"I couldn't wait to see you," she whispered, doing everything she could to pull him into her. He smelled good, he tasted good, he felt good.

His gray eyes were warm with love as he dropped kisses all over her face. "Let's get out of here. I want to talk and fuck. Not necessarily in that order. Know any cubby holes where we can hide around here, and you can ride me?"

Andromeda giggled even as her body responded to the dirty talk. "I wish, believe me. Let's just get out of here."

It took them another half hour of waiting for his suitcase to come around to baggage claim. Andromeda didn't mind waiting for it though. That suitcase told her he planned on staying for longer than a week.

They drove back through the airport traffic. It was quitting time for a lot of people so interstate 670 was bumper to bumper. Parker drove, allowing Andromeda to hold his hand and rub his thigh and whatever else she could reach. By the time they got back to her condo, Parker was fit to be tied.

"You're an evil woman," he growled as she backed into his erection in the elevator.

"Welcome back, Mr. Quinn!"

Parker gritted his teeth in her ear. "Thank you, Hampton. I'm glad to be back. How's the head?"

Parker shoved himself hard into Andromeda's rear, making her gasp and giggle.

"Oh, it's fine sir. Thank you for asking. You two have a good night and if you need anything you let me know."

"You too, Hampton. And thank you."

As soon as they exited the elevator Parker ran his hands inside her coat and beneath her blouse. He tweaked her nipples hard enough to make her gasp. Andromeda turned and hurried to the door.

They were barely inside when he caught her from behind and began kissing down the nape of her neck. "Fuck, I missed you, woman."

"I missed you too," she gasped as he hiked her skirt up her ass.

Fingers stroked her below and Andromeda's legs almost went out from beneath her. "Bed," she cried, jerking away.

She shucked her panties as she jogged to the bedroom, then her heels. He caught her as she was crawling onto the bed. "Right there," he growled.

Andromeda was on her hands and knees, bare to his sight and touch. She moaned as he ran his fingers over her again, then again and again. When he slipped a long finger inside her, she moaned, her hips shifting against his touch. "I want you inside me, Parker. You."

The sound of his zipper was loud in the room, then he was there behind her, his cock nudging her opening.

"Yes," she hissed. "Yes, please."

Parker pushed himself inside her, but he didn't have to

push very hard. She was drenched with arousal and he slid deep on the first surge. Then he stilled, his hands gripping her hips. Andromeda could feel how much he wanted her. It was there in the way he held his breath, and the way his dick moved inside her, though he was trying to stay still. His body had other plans.

Andromeda rocked back against him, making him move. She'd been waiting for weeks for this.

Parker seemed to come to the same conclusion because he began moving, hard. Their bodies slapped as he pounded into her and it was perfect. Within seconds she was arching with pleasure. Her body shattered and convulsed, but he kept going until his own body hovered on the brink. Then, with several mighty jerks, he released himself into her.

Panting, Andromeda sprawled forward. Parker still had a tight grip on her ass, so he just followed her down, their bodies still connected. He sighed as he snuggled in behind her. "Best damn homecoming ever," he told her. "No lie."

Even as her pleasure receded he was twisting her heart. What she wouldn't do to go back and welcome him home all the other times he'd returned to the States. "I love you. Parker. Welcome home. From now on I will always welcome you home."

He kissed her shoulders and her neck and ran his hand down her arm. He seemed to understand her deeper meaning. "Thank you, Andy. You have no idea how much that means to me."

IT WASN'T until over breakfast the next morning that they got around to talking.

Andromeda didn't think she could be any happier than

she already was, until he told her about Duncan's proposal. "Wait, back up a minute. He's thinking about setting up a branch in Columbus? Why?"

"Well, I asked him the same thing and apparently a lot of the guys in Denver are from back east. He knows there's a large population of veterans here and if I can prove to him that the work is here, he'll start staffing an office. Right now, I'm a one man consulting service." Parker smirked at her as he patted his thick chest. "Columbus PD has already hired me through Lost and Found to consult for them. Apparently one of the secondaries from the al Fareq case has led them to another cell, and they know they're going to require my services."

Andromeda gaped and shook her head in hopeful disbelief. "So, that means you aren't leaving?"

Grinning, Parker leaned toward her. "Not for a very long time. Months, at least, if not years. Is that okay with you?"

"Okay?" She shook her head as tears began to slide down her cheeks, but she couldn't say anything else. Her throat was too tight.

Parker seemed to understand. "I love you, Andy. I've loved you for years. Think we can get it right this time?"

She nodded her head, burying her face in his neck, too overcome with love to speak. Yes, this time they would definitely make it work. "I feel like our life has been on pause for eight years. I'm ready to start living. I love you, Parker Quinn."

I want to thank you for taking a chance on our series! We had a wonderful time working with each other and we've already received requests for more, so we'll have to see.

If you're interested in my work, you should totally sign up for my newsletter. That's where I announce EVERYTHING!

Jen's Newsletter

I have a passion for writing for the underdog and my readers feel that. I hope I made a connection with you!

Also, please be sure to leave a review! They are so important to us as authors!

The Sleeper SEALs series is a multi-author branded series which includes twelve standalone books by some of your favorite romantic suspense authors. You can check out the rest of the books in the series on our website:

www.SleeperSEALs.com/series-books or click the links below.

Susan Stoker – PROTECTING DAKOTA – 9/5/17
http://www.stokeraces.com/home.html

Becky McGraw – SLOW RIDE – 9/26/17
https://authorbeckymcgraw.com

Dale Mayer – MICHAELS' MERCY – 10/3/17
http://www.dalemayer.com

Becca Jameson – SAVING ZOLA – 10/17/17
http://www.beccajameson.com

Sharon Hamilton – BACHELOR SEAL – 10/31/17
http://sharonhamiltonauthor.com

Elle James – MONTANA RESCUE – 11/14/17
https://ellejames.com

Maryann Jordan – THIN ICE – 11/28/17
http://www.maryannjordanauthor.com

Donna Michaels – GRINCH REAPER – 12/12/17
http://donnamichaelsauthor.com

Lori Ryan – ALL IN – 1/9/18
http://loriryanromance.com

Geri Foster – BROKEN SEAL – 1/23/18
http://gerifoster.com

Elaine Levine – FREEDOM CODE – 2/6/18
https://www.elainelevine.com

J.M. Madden – FLAT LINE – 2/20/18
http://www.jmmadden.com

<<<<>>>>

ABOUT THE AUTHOR

NY Times and USA Today Bestselling author J.M. Madden writes compelling romances between 'combat modified' military men and the women who love them. J.M. Madden loves any and all good love stories, most particularly her own. She has two beautiful children and a husband who always keeps her on her toes.

J.M. was a Deputy Sheriff in Ohio for nine years, until hubby moved the clan to Kentucky. When not chasing the family around, she's at the computer, reading and writing, perfecting her craft. She occasionally takes breaks to feed her animal horde and is trying to control her office-supply addiction, but both tasks are uphill battles. Happily, she is writing full-time and always has several projects in the works. She also dearly loves to hear from readers! So, drop her a line. She'll respond.

Jennifer Loves to hear from her readers!
www.jmmadden.com
authorjmmadden@gmail.com

Grif and Kendall

SEAL's Lost Dream-Flynn

Flynn and Willow

SEAL's Christmas Dream

Flynn and Willow

Unbreakable SEAL- Max

Max and Lacey

Embattled Christmas

Reclaiming The Seal

Gabe and Julie

Loving Lilly

Diego and Lilly

Her Secret Wish

Rachel and Dean

Wish Upon a SEAL (Kindle World)

Drake and Izzy

Mistletoe Mischief

Cass and Roger

Lost and Found Pieces

Other books by J.M. Madden

A Touch of Fae

Second Time Around

A Needful Heart

Wet Dream

Love on the Line

The Billionaire's Secret Obsession

The Awakening Society- FREE

Tempt Me

If you'd like to connect with me on social media and keep updated on my releases, try these links:

Newsletter

Website

Facebook

Twitter

And of course you can always email me at authorjmmadden@gmail.com

Made in the USA
Middletown, DE
24 October 2021

50929122R00116